The Love of Dunhuang

ALSO BY YUN HUMYONG

Seom
(The Island)
1986

Buhwal-haneun Sae
(The Resurrecting Bird)
1985

Modeun Byeol-deul-eun Eumak Sori-reul Naenda
(All Stars Make Music)
1987

Wonsung-i-neun Eopda
(There Is No Monkey)
1989

Yaksok Eopneun Sedae
(A Generation Without Promise)
1990

Hyopgwei Yolcha
(Narrow Gauge Trains)
1994

Yeo-u Sanyang
(Fox Hunting)
1997

Gajang Meoli Issneun Na
(The Most Distant I)
2001

Yun Humyong

The Love of Dunhuang

Translated by
Kyung-nyun Kim Richards
Steffen F. Richards

Cross-Cultural Communications
Merrick, New York
2005

This English edition is published by arrangement
with the original Korean publisher,
Moonji Publishing Co., Seoul, Korea.

This book is published with the support of the Korea Literature Translation Institute in commemoration of Korea being the Guest of Honor at the Frankfurt Book Fair 2005.

The publisher is grateful to the KLTI for its support
and to the New York State Council on the Arts
and the National Endowment for the Arts
whose past seed grants, in part, have contributed
to making this publication possible.

Special thanks to Myunghee Kim for her invaluable
advice and assistance in arranging for the publication rights.

Published in the United States by
Cross-Cultural Communications
239 Wynsum Avenue, Merrick, NY 11566-4725/U.S.A.
Tel: (516) 868-5635 / Fax: (516) 379-1901
E-mail: cccpoetry@aol.com
www.cross-culturalcommunications.com

ISBN 0-89304-737-6
ISBN 0-89304-738-4 (pbk.)

Photograph by Song Ha-Chun

Art and Book Design by Tchouki
Hardcover binding by Frank Papp
Printed in Bulgaria

Contents

"The Love of Dunhuang"
9

"The Love of Loulan"
93

About "The Love of Loulan"
120

Translators' Acknowledgments
121

About the Translators
122

About the Author
123

The Love of Dunhuang

I awoke as usual on the same old iron bed. It was an old bed, but I could always fall into a dreamless sleep on it. Just when I was wondering how we were going to survive the winter on a cold floor, I happened to haggle with a junkman vending from a trailer cart. My girlfriend pulled at my sleeve, telling me it might be better to get a fold-up, foam-rubber mattress. Why do we need a bed for a rented room? It's not even a bed, it's just a piece of junk. I could tell she was saying these two things, just by looking at her. But when we put out the pad of thick foam rubber that we had bought at Namdaemun Marketplace and put a blanket on top, it made quite a passable bed. And that winter was especially cold. We learned, though, since the bed was so narrow and we had to cling to each other, that there was no better way to avoid the bitter cold from the stone-and-cement floor than that. We didn't have any heating bill to pay, but when we got out of bed, I felt that the dissipating warmth of the bed was like an electric meter running for nothing. Anyway, it was only short of a miracle that whoever slept on the outside never fell out of bed once.

Although my eyes were open, my head was numb from the liquor I had drunk the night before. I don't know when it started, but whenever I drink, my memory of it becomes disjointed, like pieces of a tapeworm, and slips out of my brain. It wasn't any different with my memory of being with this guy. Faint though my memory is, I have the feeling that we were singing. I can see everything as if it were on a videotape being replayed at slow speed. It was actually this guy who first brought up the singing. He said it was a new habit of his that, as soon as he has a drink, he starts singing at the top of his voice, to the annoyance of his neighbors. He even ventured a bit of self-diagnosis, saying he probably got real crazy. I said he was pretty lucky his neighbors didn't say anything. Then he grew confidential.

"No, they're not quiet. They just don't report me, because my family has been living there so long. Hey, they say it's because I haven't gotten married yet. They say I will go nuts if I keep it up. Heck, does anybody drink and sing just because they don't get married? Do they go nuts?"

"It's possible, I suppose." I responded blandly and this seemed to get him worked up even more.

"Wha … wha … wha … what? Do you know what grade the kid would be in if I had had one with that woman then?"

He was half out of his seat. I must not have been so drunk at the time, as my memory of it seems pretty intact. I also recall noticing "Dapune" conspicuously painted on the tent of our sidewalk drinkery.

"Listen, pal. Don't worry about that. That's the way it is when things are real peaceful. During the Silla Dynasty, at its peak, the sound of music in Sorabol lasted all night, isn't that true?"

"What? The Silla Dynasty?" He blinked at length, as if to ask, what kind of nonsense is this?

"So, why'd the Silla collapse?" he asked, holding up his cup.

"Who said it collapsed, kid? Silla unified the Three Kingdoms." I scoffed at him, keeping a straight face.

"It was conquered by the Goryeo Dynasty later on, you nitwit. You think the people of Goryeo sang more?"

"You sound like a Chinaman. Those weren't the same songs they sang on the battlefield."

Whenever I got together with him, we wouldn't say goodbye until we were as drunk as we could get. We drank like mad, as if we were in a race. The whole time he would mumble about how liquor was his enemy, and how it would have been better to have been born in a country like Arabia, where there is no liquor.

"You could go to work for a construction company and go over there. You could go, quit drinking, and string together four wives, couldn't you?" I said.

"That'd be great!" he chimed in, staring at me. "Bu … but, I can't understand why the word 'alcohol' comes from Arabic. How could they name something they can't even drink? What do you think? Alcohol. Good name, isn't it?"

He was nodding, as if he really didn't care about drinking, but was only drinking because of the name, "alcohol." We were both quite drunk by the time we started talking to each other like this.

"You sure as hell are going to sing a lot tonight, aren't you? Like a grasshopper. No, like the people of Silla."

This is how I teased him.

"A grasshopper?"

"Yeah. Right, kid."

When I answered him like this, pieces of my memory were starting to run away. I really can't trace everything back in detail.

"Heh, heh, heh." I thought I heard him chuckling. "Can a grasshopper sing *hyangga*? I'm talking about *hyangga*, you ignorant dodo!"

"Hyangga?"

"That's right. I'm asking you: Can a grasshopper sing *hyangga*?"

He spoke with considerable self-assurance, contrary to what I expected. Then I thought I heard him say he would sing something from the *hyangga*, but what I remember comes to a halt right here.

We must have sung Hyeon In's staccato rendering of "Ah, ahh, a moonlit night in Silla," as it still lingers in my ears and on my lips.

I only knew him for a short while in school. We were both members of the drama club. But somehow we ran into each other all the time, after we left school. He was a self-proclaimed theater-butt and wondered out loud more than a couple of times, half-jokingly, whether I wouldn't join forces with him in the theater. If it wasn't a suggestion, it was close to an appeal. It was even stronger than an appeal. He would talk as if the thing were a pastime of his whenever we met. My own view was that it was pretty odd for "a theater-buff and a non-theater-buff" to get together. What he demanded of me was that I write a play. He said he would then direct it. Knowing that I was unemployed and not doing anything, he pressured me the more, as if to seize his chance.

"You already know the answer, don't you? How the hell could I write a play? You know I don't know anything." I used to say this whenever he brought up the subject. "You are a professional writer, but I'm just an amateur. I've hardly even made up my mind to write anything. How dare you try to take advantage of a poor innocent writer like me!"

I would decline politely. Of course, declining politely was always followed by my ordering either a dish of hors d'oeuvres or a half-bottle of liquor to be paid for out of my meager wallet.

"Now that I know you are a poor innocent writer, I'm all the more tempted to come on to you. Are you really so innocent? You want to have it out, to see who wins?" He laughed.

"You dingbat."

But last night, he stuck to me like a leech, from the minute we stepped into the "Dapune House."

"The owner of this place is a Greek lady. She doesn't know how to spell, though. 'Pu' should be 'peu.' It's not the word 'to dip out,' but the Daphne of Greek myth. It should be 'Dapeune.'" He muttered about whether I was listening to him or not. Suddenly, he got serious.

He said that Daphne in Greek mythology was a beautiful nymph who fled Apollo's advances by turning into a laurel.

"Hey, when are they going to stop calling you, 'Small Props'?"

I hadn't even ordered anything to eat. I was a little surprised to hear him say "Small Props," but I wasn't entirely unhappy, either. Actually, I had shown up a few times at the drama club, but I had never done anything as part of it. The reason he called me "Small Props" was because I once had been listed as being in charge of small props. But I never knew anything about it. Having called me 'Small Props, " he started hitting below the belt with his comments. Tell me, what is unemployment like, anyway? There may not be any money in it, but isn't it better than wallowing on the floor with one eye on your girlfriend and her mood? Then he started bringing up my weaknesses. At first I thought what he was saying was the same old stuff. But this time it was different. He said I had to write. And it should be staged at the next performance.

"How can I do that?"

I had never written a play, and as far as plays were concerned, I was pretty much at a loss. But he wouldn't listen. I had never even seen a play that he directed.

"Are you gonna go on like this?"

"Why not? I have no talent. Let's stop talking about it. Why don't you tell me about your love life?"

"Huh, huh, huh. You're trying to trick me!"

While he was looking skeptical, I took the opportunity to change the subject and asked what he wanted to eat. I jutted my chin toward the wooden tray which had chicken gizzards, sea eels, sea cucumbers, and sea squirts all laid out on it. He wasn't at all interested.

"I don't care. Order anything. I am talking about something serious. It's not because you're so great that I want to work with you, stupid. You're out-to-lunch if you think that. I'm trying to help you, as a friend."

I half-listened to him and ordered a plate each of sea cucumbers and sea squirts. We usually said "anything" in a restaurant as if it were some kind of prefix, but actually we were extremely picky about what we ate. I knew good and well what he liked. Even before the food came, he began to sip his drink and to comment again on the "small props" business. According to his ridiculous reasoning, I was supposed to do something in a play in some capacity, in order to rid myself of the "small props" label. Otherwise, I would forever be known as the "small props" so-and-so. In other words, my descendants and I would both benefit if I tacked up my name as the author of a play.

"Do you want your epitaph engraved with 'Small Props' after your name?" He was stretching it, like some kid.

"You're putting me on. What's the difference whether I'm 'Small Props' or 'Large,' once I'm dead? Do you go around worrying about what your epitaph will say? Great. You're great: I've never been in charge of small props, anyway—you know that. What the hell is a 'small props' guy supposed to look like?"

Even if I hadn't been in charge of small props, my name had been printed on a program, and a few classmates of mine who knew me did call me "Small Props" as a nickname. But this nickname was given to me because of my small build and not because of the theater.

"A 'small props' face? You've got one."

"Don't make me laugh."

It didn't matter what he said, I just laughed anyway and shook my head. No doubt he wanted to work with me out of "friendship" and I should have been thankful for his suggestion, even if it "wouldn't make any money." If we could actually put on a good play, there would be no reason to run away from it. Nevertheless, to be honest, I couldn't help but feel a little nauseated by his continual use of the word "friendship."

The food arrived. He picked up one of the safety pins that were lined up neatly along the edge of the wooden tray and jabbed a slice of sea cucumber. Believing that my refusal had now been politely accepted, I started watching him. But I was wrong. He smeared some hot vinegar dip onto his slice of sea cucumber and shoved it into his mouth. He chewed it as if it were slippery somehow and then smiled mysteriously.

"I'm asking you one last time. Are you really going to have nothing to do with me, or what?" He had stopped smiling and become insistent.

He seemed certain that I could write if I wanted to. In school I used to come up with half-baked criticisms, such as on the poverty and crudeness of fictional plays, and now it had come back to haunt me.

"I'm painfully aware of how little I know and of how little talent I have."

I stood my ground. He said, "I knew you'd ..." and pushed another slice of sea cucumber into his mouth. "Even sea cucumber doesn't taste like it used to in the old days." I just stared at him, wondering what ridiculous trick he was going to pull next. For a time, he kept busy chewing the sea cucumber, munching away on it.

"I knew you would play hard to get, so I got some material together for you. I guess it's a kind of a disease to like a friend so much — a big disease," he said, with an enigmatic smile.

"Material?"

"Right."

It was all I could do to keep from laughing at that moment. Although he smiled with satisfaction as he talked, I knew from past occasions what his material was like.

"You are loaded with wonderful material, aren't you?"

In the beginning, he used to say that he was out to record material that contained dramatic elements, but later on, he went after stories of any kind. He cast his net over materials both old and new, and from both East and West. An example: the story of Jeong Yakjeon, who wrote *Jasan Eobo* (A Register of Fish from Heuksan-do Island) in 1801 while in exile on that island, and the current Japanese Emperor, Hirohito, said to have been an expert in ichthyology, arguing back and forth over ichthyological studies of the past. This was such a ridiculous story. Others were: a sequel to *The Woodcutter and the Fairy*, after the two were separated; a monologue of Napoleon on the island of St. Helena; a play about a wimpy intellectual of the Goryeo Dynasty who went to study in China during the Yuan Dynasty and took a Mongolian name, Timur (the title was supposed to be *What Happened to Jeong Timur Last Night?*); *Father's Knees*, a story about Wounded Knee, when Indians died fighting the White Men; *Love or a Turd,* a story inspired by a king of Silla who took for his queen a maiden who ate a lot and made large turds; *The Mummy Wakes Up*, a story about a magician who breathes life into mummies; etc. He had endless lists of titles, and if they had anything in common, it was that they were all taken either from history or from legend.

"This is different from everything else. It tops them all." His face was flushed with excitement, like a sea squirt's.

"You are not going to cut out another penis, are you?" I asked sarcastically, as I thought about it.

"What? A penis?" Even he had to burst out laughing, out of control, as he asked me. This was because it involved one of those fantastic stories that he had recorded not long ago. In his words, it was "indeed fantastic" material. It derived from a folk custom that is still practiced in Samcheok, along the east coast of Korea. He had this "material" written down in his notebook like sprinkled sesame seeds.

> Once there was a young girl who went down to the seashore from her village to dig clams and gather seaweed. But her basket did not fill up. A young fisherman of the village took her to a small, rocky island offshore, saying there was much more there that could be gathered up for food. The young man left the island, promising to return that evening, to bring her back to shore. There was a lot to pluck and take in. The young girl filled her basket to the brim. Evening came. But the young man who had promised to come and take her back did not come. He had just forgotten in the heat of his labors. By chance, that night was hit hard by a storm. He then remembered, but couldn't do a thing. As soon as the storm died down, he went over to the island in his rowboat. But the girl was nowhere to be found.

However, the folk customs still being practiced with this story behind them are amazing. His eyes sparkled. "As the New Year comes around, each villager whittles down a piece of wood into the shape of a phallus and hangs it on the local guardian tree, in order to console the soul of the poor young girl."

He was watching to see how I would react, wondering what I thought of it and whether or not it was interesting. I was thinking how incompatible this indigenous story was with the word "phallus," which sounded so pedantic.

"Phallus? You mean, penis?"

"Right."

He seemed pretty disappointed by my lukewarm response. To be frank, it seemed odd for a story collector of his caliber to get his mitts only now on this strange story of why penises are hung up. I got a little annoyed at him for expecting me to egg him on by telling him how amazing his story was, or the like. So I made some off-the-wall remark.

"The word 'phallus' doesn't go well with folklore. Is the story supposed to be more erudite if you use it?"

"Haven't you heard of phallic worship? They make a large penis out of stone or wood and worship it."

"I guess."

"That's what it is. It's phallic worship ..."

He seemed quite dissatisfied with me for not having said anything one way or the other about his "amazing" prize story, and for just simply latching on to a word that was unessential to the story.

"Anyway, what's the difference between saying phallic worship and penis worship? Why the hell do you have to use such a difficult word? It doesn't go with it anyhow," I said in rebuke.

"Don't get excited. You're right, you're right. It's a penis, a penis. Hey, have you got some kind of psychological problem about your thing?"

He had replied as if he had no choice but to accept what I said. But then, in a quick change of heart, he said, "Wouldn't it be great? A blunt title: 'Carving Penises.' Hell! It takes guts to puncture the psyche of modern man and catch him by surprise."

He was getting excited by his own words. I had no idea how "carving penises" would shock modern man's psyche. So I was a bit nonplussed. He seemed to think "carving penises" was something like "cracking nuts" from the *Nutcracker* ballet by Tchaikovsky, and it made me laugh.

"Guts? Man, you got 'em!" I was being sarcastic, but he didn't seem to notice. On the other hand, his confidence was improving.

"It's true we're stuck with the notion that Chinese words are more dignified and respectable." He said this as if "carving penises" had hit the mark in his own psyche. His hot temperament made him seem flippant, but, actually, he knew a lot about a lot of things and was also quite sincere in many ways.

He continued with a whole slew of questions, at random: Why can't Koreans say "penis" or "vagina" when they need to? Is it because Korea has been known as The Polite Nation of the East? Why is it any better to use the Chinese word meaning "phallus" or "vulva"? Are the words penis and vagina obscene, but phallus and vulva are not? What do "xx" and the symbol for multiplication mean in books? Why do linguists say that the Korean word for "vagina" has a southern provenance but cannot clarify the etymology of the Korean word for "penis." If the Korean word for vagina has a Polynesian origin, are they telling us that Koreans didn't have a word for "vagina" before that? And is it possible that "penis" and "vagina" have separate etymological origins?

He brought up all these questions rather academically.

"From my simplistic point of view," he began, oratorically, "if the word for vagina is definitely of Polynesian origin, then, I think, the word for penis also ought to have a southern origin." He concluded with a note of confidence.

"They say that the pieces of wood have to be cut to shape and hung so as to pacify the spirit of the girl. The fishermen will then have a good harvest. It's a rite for a good catch."

I was going to needle him about what kind of a girl would find a penis so interesting, but I didn't. I guess it was because of his enthusiasm for the subject, and because I could imagine the desperation of the fishermen that lay behind this strange custom. Anyway, he was wondering whether it wouldn't be a fantastic idea to write a play reeking with local color, with this strange custom as its backdrop.

"Yep, you're right. It would be fantastic. Listen, pal. Just because something is exotic doesn't mean that it makes a good play. If it was a 'rite for a good catch,' it's more like poetry. Wasn't poetry meant as a prayer for a good catch when ancient people began going out on hunting and fishing expeditions?" I was being somewhat noncommittal. I continued: "I think the true artist of today should be rooted in the little things of ordinary, everyday life, rather than in something so strange and bizarre." This sure dampened his exuberance.

This was what his "Carving Penises" was all about.

I couldn't keep from laughing when I heard he had brought even more "fantastic" material for me. I knew pretty well how worthless his "material" was. Nonetheless, I must admit that my curiosity was aroused, and I wondered what outlandish thing he wanted to do next. He pulled out some crumpled pages of a magazine. There was a glossy page of photographs and a few pages of text on bonded white paper.

"How come it seems so elaborate?" At my jest, he flushed even more.

Taking his papers, he spread them out on the counter. "This is an article about Donhwang." He became serious.

"Donhwang?" I asked, as I brought the cup to my lips.

"Yeah, it's Dunhuang in Chinese, which is in western China. It's an old Buddhist historical site. They say there are more than a thousand temples in the caves. They are called the Mogao Caves."

I remember having read about Dunhuang in several books which I had skimmed through, but everything was kind of vague. Muttering to myself that not just the sea cucumbers but also the sea squirts had al become westernized, I pushed a slice of sea-squirt into my mouth. He had just been about to jump eagerly into a new exposition, but my out-of-the-blue comment on the sea squirt seemed to deflate him.

"Never mind westernized or Japanized, you bum. Dunhuang is an important heritage for us. There's a tremendous amount of Buddhist statues and murals in the caves. There's even an academic discipline called Dunhuangology."

"What's that got to do with us?"

"That's just it. No matter how important something is, it's meaningless unless it's relevant to us." He was beginning to liven up.

"I don't think this thing has anything to do with us."

It was not that I was unaware of the overall view that everything on earth has some connection to our life, for I was familiar with expressions like "global village." Thinking that he might be getting to some such vacuous, thin story, I replied rather unenthusiastically.

"I don't know what degree of relevance you're talking about, but from my simplistic point of view, it will vary depending on what we make of it."

"Indeed, that is simplistic."

"Hey, Sea Squirt-Small Props, this is no joke, get me?"

He roared and then started putting me down with one phrase after another, things he had heard who-knows-where. He accused me of not having any sense of mission regarding our culture, of being saturated with a regressive point of view even though I was not even thirty, of not having a vision for the future, and of leading a cancerous existence. I found it amusing that he would mobilize every old cliché to give expression to his anger toward me.

"You're right. Even when you tear someone apart, you have to be so damned literary!" I cajoled him.

"You've got to listen. You have to hear how Donhwang is related to us. You've heard of Hyecho? His *Record of a Journey to the Five Kingdoms of India* was found there." He was raising his voice.

"The Silla monk, Hyecho? How could his book have been found there?"

"That's why I am telling you about this."

He had that I-told-you-so look on his face. But even that seemed like something I had seen in a book before.

"Look at th … this."

He pointed to the photographs spread out on the wooden counter. It was the page I had been looking at from the beginning, with a photo of the interior of a grotto. There was a gilded Buddha in the middle, with Buddhist monks and Bodhisattvas surrounding it. Beneath the seat of the Buddha were the benefactors, the demons, and some lions. Along the four sides were a thousand Buddhas, and on the ceiling were the Flying Heavenly Beings.

"From the Repository of Scriptures, the cave known as Zangjingdong, the French archeologist, Paul Pelliot, removed a huge amount of relics, and Hyecho's book was among them. By the way, I heard that the cave was discovered completely by accident."

Compared to what he had put together up to this point, this story seemed to have a little class. Responding for the first time, I said only, "Is that right?" and just continued to listen. Even if Hyecho's travels had been discovered among the archeological finds, I could get no real sense that it had any direct bearing on my life. Gansu Province in China is a long way from Seoul. The grotto in the picture had been restored and refurbished, and it was difficult to believe the excavator's account that the whole thing had been found abandoned in some bleak desert.

"Not only was Hyecho's book discovered there, but he is said to have actually stayed there for a long period, to write the book."

I was reminded of *Following the Road Taken* by Hyecho, a book that the Buddhist monk, Jihyeon—known affectionately as "Gwaneum the Hairy"—wrote after he traveled to the West. But I wasn't thinking about its contents. Instead, a phrase I had heard somewhere — "In India, surviving and seeking the truth are one and the same, as when one is forced to drink one's own urine, traveling out under the hot sun" — was stuck in my head, and I couldn't get rid of it. When I saw the obviously exaggerated and even comical images of the lions of the cave, I wondered if it were Manjusri, who rode on the back of a lion.

Originally, there were more than a thousand caves in Dunhuang, but there are only about six-hundred remaining today. Of these, about 492 contain statues and murals of Buddha. The caves consist of two kinds: temple and complex. The temple caves did not have monks' quarters, whereas the complex caves did. This kind of grotto originated in India, and must have served as the model for Seokkuram, in Gyeongju, Korea.

According to his grand scheme, his play would be staged in Dunhuang. As the play opens, the scene will have Hyecho entering in his Zen meditation in the cave. This would augment the solemn beauty of the play. The story would deal with Hyecho's love, but the title of the play would be *The Love of Donhwang.* Now wouldn't that make a great play?

"What d'you think, huh?" He was going to go on *ad infinitum.*

I interrupted him: "What are you talking about? What did Hyecho love and how? There's no hint of that."

Now his complexion was changing. He clicked his tongue a couple of times and began pointing his finger at me and talking about my "lack of imagination" and my "absence of dramatic sense," etc.

"You nitwit. Can't you think of anything else besides a motel room when I'm talking about love? 'The Love of Donhwang' is not that at all. I want to deal with how *eros* sublimates and becomes *agape*."

He was getting pretty agitated now. Even though he insisted that the absence of any indication of a love affair would not pose any problem for the main thing he was trying to do, he proposed enhancing the story of Hyecho's pursuit of enlightenment by including a heartrending love affair with a foreign woman.

"That's what I would call the victory of true love. Can't you see?"

"I'm not sure."

"You're hopeless. Go home and think about it with your hand over your heart. 'The Love of Donhwang' is meant to show that the true nature of love is really a fight against oneself. Now isn't this a goo context to put it in?"

I had no idea what the nature of his "nature" was. Anyhow, I knew how he could get all worked up and then calm down on his own after a few days, so I didn't even need to reply.

"How about the love of 'Don Juan' instead of 'Donhwang' and talk about how Don Juan took his women?" I was being sarcastic.

"What? Don Juan? The love of Don Juan?"

"Yeah. Don't you know, the Spaniard? They say he seduced any woman who came his way. To put it in your terms: Why not talk about the nature of *eros* by depicting the story of his love affairs?"

He seemed only a bit disconcerted that Donhwang should be mixed up with Don Juan, but he was obviously ticked off.

"Anyway, go home and think about it, seriously. If Donhwang doesn't seem right, Dunhuang will be okay, too." He folded the magazine article, stuck it in my pocket, and called out for another bottle of liquor, even though there was more than a half-bottle still left. He downed a few more drinks. What makes you drunk is not so much how much you drink but how fast. I kept up with him and got pretty soused in no time. While we were yelling how we'd "pour ourselves all the liquor in the Dapune," he was slurring his words.

♥

I could hear my girlfriend in the other room setting the table, under pressure to make it to work on time. I staggered out of bed and checked my jacket pocket to see if the magazine article was still there. My memory of how I got home was a complete blank, but the article was in my pocket, neatly folded.

"It should be 'The Love of Dunhuang' ... What a hangover...." Mumbling to myself, I took out the article and flung myself back on the bed.

♥

About 25 kilometers southeast of the town of Dunhuang, in the province of Gansu, lies an extensive mountain range, the Mingsha Shan. It is 4000 kilometers from Beijing. This would make it exactly 10,000 *li*. The desolate and majestic Mingsha Shan is sandstone, and when you step on it, it crumbles; but the mountain range is steep and when you go up on it, you can hear the wailing of the sand. On its eastern slope, which is right out in the middle of the desert, is a group of caves that were constructed over the course of a thousand years and through ten different dynasties, in a variety of styles. These caves are known as the Mogao Caves.

The caves, which are also called the Caves of the Thousand Buddhas, show strong influences from the countries bordering China on the west in the earlier ones, but gradually became Chinese in style, and, with the Tang Dynasty, came to epitomize the essence of Chinese art. The first excavations occurred in 1905. Before this, one day in 1898, a Taoist monk named Wang Yuanlu, who kept watch over the caves, was having a scribe copy some papers. He noticed that the smoke from a cigarette which the scribe was smoking was being sucked into a crack in the wall. He inspected the crack. There was something that didn't seem natural. He immediately broke into the wall and found a large cache of old documents, sutras, and paintings. There was no way of keeping this news from spreading abroad. The Great Powers of the world, who were hell-bent on expanding their hegemony over central Asia, plundered these treasures: the Russian party of [Vladimir] Obruchev came in 1905, the British party of [Marc Aurel] Stein the next year, and the French party of [Paul] Pelliot the year following that. Later the [Kōzai] Ōtani party from Japan added to it. Dunhuangology was born from the stud of stolen archaeological artifacts from Dunhuang.

Of the 492 caves that contain sculptures or paintings, the majority were made during the Tang Dynasty. Others were made during the Sui Dynasty, the Wei, the Five Kingdom Period, and the Western Shia, Yuan, and Ching Dynasties, and they show a great diversity. With regard to how the caves came to be, there are three theories: one, that the first were made before 303 B.C., during the reign of Hui Di of the Chin; second, that they were made fifty years later, during the Eastern Chin, in the ninth year of the reign of Ying Hwa; and, third, that a monk name Le Jun made the first one in A.D. 366, in the second year of the reign of Jian Yuan. Anyway, they all go back to the fourth century.

The painted statues stored in the 492 caves number 2,415 pieces, and if we were to place all the murals together, side by side, they would measure five meters high and 25 kilometers long. The statues were made of clay, and the reason why is because the stone in the area is an aggregate. The murals were painted after the walls had been mudded. They made the statues by first binding wood tightly together with straw ropes. This became the frame. A mixture of clay, hemp cloth, and sand was then used to give it shape. It was finished with a coat of white clay and then painted or gilded. The earlier statues were destroyed along with their caves, but the oldest known to us was made during the Northern Liang period, around the first half of the fifth century.

The statues of this period show strong influences from Indian and other western styles, and these influences continue through the period of the Northern Wei, whose forces destroyed those of the Northern Liang. These influences altered, and a true Chinese style developed during the Northern Ji, Northern Chou, and into and through the Sui and Tang periods. Especially during the Tang Dynasty, the expansion of national power and the flourishing of Buddhist art favored the creation of many masterpieces. The same was also true for the murals. During the Northern Liang period, Indian and other western influences ran deep, but by the Tang Dynasty, realistic painting reached its peak: Splendid tantric paintings depict images of an ideal world which is both beautiful and mysterious.

I gave everything a once-over, but my eyes became riveted on one painting. For it seemed so familiar to me. I was wondering why there was a hunting scene in the picture when it had presumably been painted by monks. I mumbled to myself, "This is strange. This is just like the hunting scene found on a wall of the Goguryeo tomb...." The painting was on the ceiling of a cave made during the Western Wei period. It depicted a warrior on horseback aiming an arrow at a tiger, in a valley where deer were on the run. Unlike in the Goguryeo mural, the horse looked more like a wild boar, and the tiger seemed too rounded, like a dragon, but the vitality of the painting seemed comparable.

♥

"Are you awake? Why did you get so drunk last night? Do you remember what happened?"

In no time, my girlfriend had brought the round plastic table into the room. As I am almost an amnesiac when it comes to remembering things, my heart sank a little when she asked, for I was afraid I might have done something awful.

"What?"

"You kept repeating things, like Don Juan, Hyecho, Wounded Knee—all of which didn't make any sense. I couldn't figure it out."

I turned furtively away from her, still lying in bed. Considering how sarcastic I felt about my friend's "material," I felt wretched that I myself had been repeating what he had said, in my stupor.

"And what was it that the young girl was after?"

Yet more trouble.

"Get me some water."

"Are you changing the subject?"

It wasn't that I wanted to change the subject. I was thirsty.

"It's right there, right next to you."

The teakettle was on the small wooden box next to the bed. I turned over, raised the teakettle, and practically drank it dry.

"You're not having an affair with someone, are you?"

"An affair?"

"Then what the hell was that about Don Juan and the young girl being after something?"

There was a bad taste in my mouth. I wished I could have said something to squelch her, but I was loathe to think about what might have happened last night. So I just held back and ended up fudging my answer, saying it must have been something general about young women these days behaving in such-and-such a fashion. Although she had brought up the subject, it was obvious that my girlfriend wasn't really suspicious.

"Aren't you going to eat something?"

She was pressing me.

"I don't feel like it. You go ahead: You're the one who has to go to work."

"The doctor told me to fast. I guess I will just have a bowl of soup later."

She wasn't at all interested in eating. She was just busy getting ready to go out. This was the day she was going to stop by the hospital. I felt slightly nauseated, and my stomach was a little upset. I kept turning over.

"So what's a wounded knee?"

She was sitting on the floor putting on her stockings. She seemed to want to break the silence.

"You sure are hassling me this morning, do you know that?"

"You are a fine one to talk. You were the one who begged and clung to me last night, to get me to listen."

As soon as she brought up "last night," I lost my steam. Since I had no idea what I had done, I should have just felt grateful that she wasn't going beyond that. Silently kicking myself, I simply waited for her to get out.

"Your father was an Indian? I didn't understand what you were saying at all ..."

My girlfriend seemed to be teasing me. As usual, it was that "material" of his that was causing me all this trouble. He said that the American Indians were a branch of the Mongols that had crossed over to the continent and that "Apache" was derived from *abeoji*, which "father" in Korean. He went on to elaborate his hope that "Father's Knees" would be a play about the tragedy of the Indians that occurred at Wounded Knee. I don't know why I had to repeat, in my drunkenness, all those nondescript and vague ideas that he had brought up. It was enough to make me weep.

"I was saying that the American Indians came from Asia. They are Mongolian. The name Apache originated from the Korean word, *abeoji*." I didn't want to be bothered anymore and didn't care what she thought. So I had just blurted it out.

"Then why were you so serious about it yesterday? You were carrying on about how your Indian father had died and how your wounded knee was weeping, and on and on."

"What? My wounded knee was weeping?"

"Yeah."

"Umm ..."

She even smiled briefly. I thought to myself, what a complete fool I must have been, and the thought nauseated me. I pretended to be deep in thought, as if to show how serious it all was. But she wasn't even looking my way. In addition to resenting her probing of every little thing I felt compelled to assume an air of justification for my behavior last night. So I opened my mouth.

"You know what Wounded Knee is? Wounded Knee is spelled w, o, u, n, d, e, d – 'wounded' — and k, n, e, e – 'knee.' It means 'injured knee.' It's a place-name. It's the place where some Indians fought bitterly against the whites. Since they all died there, it's like a cemetery." Like a parrot, I was repeating what my friend had said.

"So what's that got to do with you?" she asked, as if the whole thing were off-the-wall. Since I had responded the same sort of way to my friend when he told me about it, things had now gotten pretty twisted.

"Boy, you are sure getting on my nerves. When the Master speaks, Children and Women are supposed to be quiet."

"Lucky you." She didn't even blink. I felt my insides churning all over the place.

"Be quiet! I am not talking to you just to hear you talk back. Listen. I told you that Indians were Mongols!" I raised my voice so much, the veins on my neck popped out. But she still had the same dumb look:

"Yeah? ... So?"

"It's because you are so frustrating that I drink and keep on talking."

"Go ahead and talk. I was late to work yesterday, too."

She hurriedly looked in the mirror, covered the small table of food with some newspaper, and zipped up the vinyl wardrobe.

"I'm talking about the Mongols. Who are the Mongols? Huh? Who are they?"

I didn't know what I was doing.

"They must be Indians, I guess...," she answered without thinking. I became exasperated and sat up with a jerk.

"What? The Mongols are Indians?"

"Why? Am I wrong?"

"Did I ever say that? Did I ever say that the Mongols were Indians?"

"Calm down. You just said it a moment ago, didn't you?" She even gave me a dirty look.

"You're killing me." I slapped my chest with the palm of my hand.

"What's that for?" She was as cool as she could be.

"Look, pay attention. Okay. Who are the Mongols? Be clear about it."

I raised her chin with the back of my hand and, turning it toward me, pressed her for an answer.

"Aren't they Indians?"

It was useless. I should have just turned my back on her when she brought up what had happened last night. I had lost my steam.

"Pay attention. You know the bluish spots on babies' butts? Do you know what they are? They're called Mongolian Spots, because they show up in the Mongol race. We are Mongolian. We are. You have to pay attention to me when I speak."

It was really embarrassing. I had never expected our conversation to go off-track like this. But by now I couldn't help myself.

"Didn't you say that already? I heard everything you said."

"Good. Then what did I say just now? What did I say about the Mongol race?"

I was pressing her with these questions.

"You said, that's what we are."

"Good. Wait a minute. Then, are you telling me that we're Indians?"

She blinked, wondering whether she had been goaded into a trap. Then she denied again ever having said that.

"Why … didn't you say the Mongolians were Indians?"

"You said so, didn't you?" my girlfriend retorted, looking completely confused.

"That's why I said, you have to pay attention. I said the Indians were Mongolian, but I never said that the Mongolians were Indians."

"The Indians are Mongolian but the Mongolians are not Indians?"

"You got it."

I smacked my lips a couple of times. It was all my fault that I had gone into all of this. I lost interest in talking about it any further. I hadn't wanted to go into it from the beginning. It was his "material," and I wasn't interested in any of it, no matter what the story was. If I had gone on, I would have had to say something like, "All Indians are Mongolian, but not all Mongols are Indians," etc., and have to explain it as though it were some study in logic. I dreaded that. So I stopped. I was just happy she hadn't brought up any more ridiculous talk about weeping and wounded knees. She must have figured that there wasn't much more to listen to, anyway.

"Are you going to meet me this evening?" she asked as she put on her watch. I remembered we were supposed to have dinner together after she quit work early and stopped at the hospital.

"Sure."

Sitting on the bed and lighting a cigarette, I nodded "of course." She opened the door and turned to me.

"Where shall we meet?"

"Well...," I paused and thought for a moment about a few places. Then I said, "At the Injured Knee."

"Haven't you finished that story yet?"

"Of course, I'm finished."

"I have to hurry now."

"Living together is a tomb in the midst of life. We die fighting. You know the tearoom where we used to meet, dying to live together." mumbled it without laughing.

"Fine. See you at the "Knee." Is seven okay?"

"Sure."

My girlfriend tottered as she put on her shoes. She said she had bought the wrong thing and they were very uncomfortable. After getting them on, she poked her head in the room. "What's so great about the Injured Knee? Don't be late." She stuck her tongue out at me in a flash and then vanished as though she had fled.

The hours after she left were always upside down. I would either go back to bed or fall into a daydream about the uncertain future. Either way, it was pathetic. I flung myself again onto the iron bed. I had felt better when I was having that useless exchange with my girlfriend, but now the back of my head felt numb and it made me sink down heavily. I also felt dopey. I kept still until I fell asleep, and I slept hard for a long time, going in and out of dreams. It was afternoon, but there was still a lot of time left. If I had to go out, I would have to meet with my friend before going to the tearoom.

♥

My friend was watching a videotape with a few of his drama students in the so-called rehearsal space that had been made by putting up several sheets of plywood in a corner of the office space that his brother-in-law had rented for his business.

"Oh, it's you. Can you wait a minute?" Having said this, he quickly turned back toward the screen. Obviously, they were all quite engrossed in it. As I grew curious and began glancing at what they were watching, he said, "Bongsan," and smiled, showing all his teeth. It was the Bongsan Mask Dance. At their back, hovering over the line of students who were glued to the screen, I took out a cigarette and lit it.

"So, you got home OK yesterday?" He turned to look at me.

"Of course."

"Considering that you are here today, you must have been pretty impressed by what I told you yesterday. Were you?" He grinned broadly, looking at me and then the screen by turns.

"I have a date with my old lady and it's a while off," I said indifferently.

"What d'you mean, 'old lady,' when you're not even married? Anyway, you see her all the time at home, don't you? Did she run away?"

"Yeah, she ran away."

I had seen the video of the Bongsan Mask Dance three or four times since I began seeing him. Sometimes I saw only the first part, and at other times I saw the last part. I don't know where he got his students, but judging from how they stared at the screen, they seemed serious and even a little embarrassed.

Dressed in a three-flap jacket with a red body and green sleeves, which he wore over a pair of red pantaloons, his bells jingling, Chwibari, the Drunkard, was performing, tilting his head from side to side. On his orange mask, which was painted with black-and-white spots, there were seven large bumps. Judging from what he was doing with the Old Master and the Young Shaman, it was the scene when he entices the Young Shaman and seduces her. Whenever he gets near the Young Shaman, the Old Master hits him. Chwibari glares at the Old Master like a ghost or an ogre, and their fighting grows more intense. At last, he drives away the Old Master and takes the Young Shaman. She was dressed in a red skirt and a jacket with colored sleeves and long white ends that covered her hands. Her chignon was held in place by a long hairpin, and she was crowned with a head ornament, the *jokdori*. Against her white face, her red lips looked especially sensual.

"Have you eaten lunch yet?" He asked, perhaps sorry he had made me wait.

"You know what time it is."

"Anyway, wait just a bit more. This thing with the kids will be over in a minute."

I had to give him credit for his enthusiasm. I thought it hadn't been long ago that he had first become interested in the Mask Dance, but here he was, already teaching his students about it.

"Now, let's have a look at this dance."

I looked at the screen as he had directed and saw the Buddhist Monk with his round face and his garment dyed ink-black.

"Isn't that the Buddhist Monk?" someone asked, to show off what he knew.

"Right. It's the Buddhist Monk. His is the most important role in the Bongsan Mask Dance. So let's watch him. The dance he is going to perform is called *The Summons*, which means that he is going to *call out the rhythms,* as he is the first to start the dancing. He will display all the basic movements.

There was a pause on screen for a little while, and then things started to move again, slowly. All eyes were riveted on the screen.

"This is one of the basic movements in the Bongsan Mask Dance. See? His legs are spread apart."

The Monk had his legs spread to the width of his shoulders and his hands raised to shoulder height and covered by the white extensions of his sleeves. His two feet were splayed, as they naturally would be in their neutral position.

"This is the ready position. When the first beat comes down with a tum ..." In contrast to my friend's composure, his "kids" were tense and awkward.

Standing on his tiptoes, the Monk stretched out his entire body as though he were soaring, and then twisted his body to the right. He swung his left arm and the right in full circles. The next moment, he bent his knees and lowered himself, bringing down his waist and shoulders to their proper places. Drawing circles with his arms, he came forward obliquely.

"This was the movement for the first beat. Next, tum..., when the second beat comes down ..."

The Monk repeated movements similar to those of the first dance.

"Since the second beat is weak, he turns slightly. He bends his knee even further and settles almost to the ground."

At the second beat, he was to straighten his legs and return to the ready position of the beginning.

"No matter the kind of Mask Dance, the movements of *The Summons* are important, even though they seem simple, because the musical accompaniment will follow. It's like a cue during a play."

It didn't look as though his instruction of the "kids" would finish soon, even though he said it would.

Ever since he had graduated from college five years ago, my friend had been living an uncertain life as a director without really directing much of anything. In his meandering life, if there was any gradual change at all, it was that he began to direct more original plays from translated works, like *Our Town* by Thornton Wilder and *The Glass Menagerie* by Tennessee Williams. And now he was broadening his work to include the Mask Dances. He was concerned about, and objected to, the practices of college mask-dance classes in which humor and satire were exploited, taking advantage of the anonymity of the Mask Dance, to express criticisms of the world. He asserted that the reason masked dancers could point a finger and hurl curses at upper-class noblemen was because dancers were given tacit acquiescence and protection by the upper-class men. So, the Mask Dance was originally used as a tool for a highly advanced form of reconciliation rather than of criticism. He therefore insisted that the inheritance and development of the Mask Dance today ought to proceed from a positive outlook. Naturally, the purposes of college dance activities, and his way of looking at them could not help but be on a collision course. This did not mean that he was devoting himself entirely to the Mask Dance, either. When I suggested to him that he place himself under the tutelage of some dance master, he just quietly grinned and said nothing.

"Now, let's review the primary movement of the Monk. Remember that this single movement is a splendid dance of masculine exuberance and is based on a harmony between his devilish mask and the rhythm of a witty dialogue."

The Monk appeared with a Lion on the screen.

"Don't watch the Lion. Watch the Monk. Now, beat one."

The Monk lifted his right knee to a ninety-degree angle, pointing his toes upward, and spread his arms out at shoulder height. He jumped, twisting towards the right. Just as my friend had said, the dancer shook his mask, causing it to tremble so as to augment the monstrousness of it. Twirling the white extension of his right sleeve behind his head, he threw it forwards. His right and left arms formed a diagonal line. The Lion came and went during the scene.

"Next, beat two."

The Monk straightened up and brought his foot down. His right hand went to the back and his left hand to the front. He brought both arms to his sides, shifted his weight to his right foot, and was ready for the next movement.

"Don't look at the Lion. Now, beat three."

His left knee raised in a right angle, toes pointing up, arms raised to shoulder level, and turning his body to the left, he jumped. His mask trembled. He twirled the white extension of his sleeve behind his head and threw it forward. His right and left arms formed a diagonal line.

"The last beat, beat four."

The Monk returned to his original position and brought down his leg. His left hand moved to the back and his right came to the front. He brought both arms to his sides, shifted his weight to the left leg, and was ready for the next move.

"You saw it, didn't you? Beats three and four are the opposite of beats one and two."

While mindlessly watching the screen, I found myself feeling sad without really knowing why. It might have been his enthusiasm. I almost felt as though it was he himself who was on the TV, he who was demonstrating the slow dance-movements, mask on his face. But it wasn't just that. I sat down on a chair in the corner. Why was the Mask Dance making me sad? I had never felt this before. If the masks were meant to dispel evil and promote joyfulness, there was no reason why I should have felt sad about it. Nevertheless, regardless of whether the mask was of a rough-and-tumble male or a coquettish female, their faces were all sad. Was it anonymity that made them sad? Perhaps. I was thinking along these lines, inhaling smoke from a cigarette deep into the pockets of my lungs when suddenly I thought of a lion, a lion wandering sadly around between monks. That's right. A picture of a lion was also painted on a wall in the Dunhuang caves.

When I first saw the Mask Dance, I had marveled at the Lion. The fact that a lion, which does not exist in Korea, could be mixed in with people in such a friendly way was enough to disturb my sense of order. One might say that I was confused because of the amazing attraction of the exotic. I would not feel the same way about monkeys. All I know is what I had heard from frequenting his studio, but the Lion with the flowing mane appears not only in the west coast towns of Bongsan, Gangnyeong, and Girin in Hwanghae-do Province, but also in the outdoor plays of Suyeong and the Five-Clown Plays of Tong-yeong, in Gyeongsang-do Province. In addition, there is the Lion Play of Bukcheong. But I have to add a few words about this latter.

The first time I ever saw a Lion was not in his studio. It was much before, before I knew anything to speak of about them. The first Lion was in a Bukcheong play. My father had been born and raised in Bukcheong. To be more precise, my father was born in Cho-ri, in New Town of Bukcheong. He was so fun-loving and so nostalgic about the hometown he had left that once, when a group of entertainers who had fled North Korea were performing the Lion Dance of Bukcheong, he took me to see it. It was quite an exciting performance. The Lion had a square face and a colorful body. The musicians, dressed in traditional costume with red, blue, or yellow sashes and hats, played flutes and drums.

The Lion danced as though it were afloat. Several masked dancers came out and circled round the Lion. It was much later, when I was frequenting my friend's studio, that I learned the identities of these dancers. They were: the Nobleman, the Head Monk, the Female Entertainer, the Hunchback, and the Dancing Boys. The Lion did tricks, too. He stood up straight and performed tricks with his paws. He pretended to catch and eat prey. At the end, after falling down, he got up again and performed an extensive set, dancing with the others. The show then finished. At that moment, my father picked me up and sat me on the back of the Lion. I was shocked out of my wits. I knew full well that there was a man inside, but I kicked and struggled against it.

"Hey, Uncle! Your father wants you to have a long, long life!"

Even though I was young, I had been addressed this way because my name indicated that the generation I belonged to in the family was ahead of his generation. My father had sat me on the back of the Lion, that I might live a long life. However, he himself died of hypertension even before he reached sixty. Was this because he had never been sat on a Lion before?

I finally asked my friend the long-unasked question: Why the Lion when there are no lions in our country?'

"Heh, heh. It's not a lion." He seemed tickled.

"What do you mean, not a lion?"

"You see it as a lion. But it's not a lion. It's a human being. Only its shape has been borrowed. That's what symbolism is."

What he said was true enough since there was a person behind the Lion's mask. I guess that such a straight-forward and simple point of view does provide high symbolic meaning to an otherwise confusing situation. Anyhow, according to my friend, the Lion in the Bukcheong Mask Dance is unique, because it plays a main role, unlike in other cases.

My friend's remark that the Lion wasn't a lion was meant as a joke, but it shocked me nonetheless in no small way. A real lion would never dance with people, and therefore his answer was unmistakably true. But I was still shocked. He was treating me like a kindergartner, and so I had to seek out the answers to my questions on my own.

♥

The Lion Play originally came from India. It was introduced to Korea during the Three Kingdom period and was enjoyed by the people of Silla as one of the Five Accomplishments. It was called the San-ye. The other accomplishments were the Geumhwan, the Woljeon, the Daemyeon and the Sokdok. Unfortunately, there remain no detailed records concerning these entertainments. Geumhwan was a game of catch played with a metal ball; Woljeon was an entertainment based on impersonation, an amusing mime using masks; Daemyeon was also a Mask Dance; and Sokdok was a Mask Dance, which was said to have originated in a country named Sogd, in a region near Tashkent and Samarkand. Except for the Geumhwan, the game played with a metal ball, everything else was a masked dance. These dances later evolved into the Sandae Variety Entertainments of the Goryeo Period, and still later into the Year-End Variety Entertainments of the Joseon Dynasty. In other words, the Five Accomplishments of the Silla period became the foundation for the masked dances, into which the joys and sorrows, and the hopes and disappointments of the Korean people became condensed.

During the transition from the Joseon period to the Japanese colonial period, there was, I found out, a woman named Geum-ok, who figured in the formation of the Mask Dance. She was a real person. She played an important part in the formation of the Gangnyeong Mask Dance, which was one of the West Coast Mask Dances and the Mask Dance of Hwanghae-do Province. Geum-ok was an entertainer, a *gisaeng*, of the West Coast Governor's office and had outstanding talent in song and dance. But after the Japanese annexation of Korea, the Governor's office was closed and she moved to Galmoro in Gangnyeong. There she drew people from the vicinity and started teaching dance. This is how the Gangnyeong Mask Dance acquired an authentic style. While tracing the story of her life, I came across the story of a man which now follows. I plunged into it and was like a zombie until the wee hours of the morning.

♥

A man was running away from something. This was because he had killed someone. The motive for the killing was based on the fact that his younger sister had committed suicide by taking arsenic. That night the owls hooted more sadly than ever. His sister had cursed this someone as she breathed her last. It was he who had forcefully raped her. No matter how humiliated she had been, her brother had desperately hoped that she would not die, but it was to no avail. She died leaving the hooting of the owls as her rite of exorcism. He gritted his teeth. As it was, he thought he could not tolerate the other's wantonness. When the times had changed and the Japanese had come in droves, this other man had become their running dog, pushing people around brazenly. He had been arrogant and his talent for taking people's property had thrived, too. And then, he had pestered the man's younger sister with unwanted advances.

The man waited for him at night and killed him with a single thrust. Afterwards, he felt no remorse at having killed someone, but only relief that he had done what he had to do. He had no regrets. Now that he was the only one left, he didn't care if he died, since he had been able to take revenge against his sister's enemy. The moon shone brightly that night. He went home, concealing himself at the edges of the moonlight, but had to take off immediately without even attending to his sister's corpse.

As he was leaving, he looked at the picture of Cheo-yong, son of the Dragon King and protector of the people against evil forces in Silla legends, which was on the wall over the doorway. His father had painted it and hung it there. His younger sister had been quite fair, unlike the daughter of a day-laborer, her father. He thought it was a misfortune that she should have been so pretty in the first place. If she hadn't been so pretty, she wouldn't have had to die so suddenly. Just then, he heard a song coming forth from a corner of his heart: *O little one, you who are so good. Though the neighbor's won't go to sleep, mine is deep in slumber.* Are the days that have passed only relayed to us through a song like this? His eyes closed, he reminisced over days gone by, and felt that time itself had been cursed, for having been cut short prematurely. What pain there is in losing one's child ahead of oneself! The older a person is who has seen painful things in his life, the more heartbroken he is after such a loss. This brokenheartedness accumulates and becomes a deep, irreversible illness of the heart.

"Hoot … hoot."

He heard an owl hooting far in the distance. Whenever he heard an owl hoot, he was reminded of the many years he had been unable to sleep thinking of Geum-ok. As her reputation as an accomplished *gisaeng* grew ever greater, the hooting of an owl gave him even greater pain. Every year, their hooting announced the arrival of Dan-o, the fifth of May by the lunar calendar. He felt nothing special even when the barley plants were harvested and taken out of the field, and spring was in full sway. But when the long hooting of the owls could be heard above the roof, he became anxious. It wasn't because his wife had died young. Though he missed Geum-ok, he was used to it and had been used to it for a long time.

"Hoot. Hoot …"

He listened as the hooting of the owls, which could be heard above the sounds of gnawing made by the mice, etched Geum-ok's face in the pitch darkness. Etched in this way, her face seemed unerasable, as though it were a lotus flower etched in stone. He couldn't remember what year it had been. But he couldn't forget that, once, one night, the leader of the Mask Dance troupe had held her in his arms. It had happened as she was gaining fame as a great *gisaeng*. That Dan-o Day, when the dancers were excitedly showing off their skills and the field for the dance was stirring with round after round of dancers, he could not have imagined that Geum-ok would be presented to the top dance troupe as a prize.

At the time, he still thought of Geum-ok as a little child with sniffles beneath the portrait of Cheo-yong. But such was how the inevitable happened. That night, Geum-ok was sacrificed to the middle-aged head of the dance troupe. This was, in a way, a kind of premature bereavement. The Mask Dance that day had been particularly rousing.

A Lion, his costume made of bamboo, white muslin, and paper, came out and performed the long dances of the Playboy and the Shaman set to folk music with shamanistic rhythms. Following the Lion's dance, Monkey, wearing a red mask with white and gold spots, appeared. He wore a red jacket with blue sleeves and red pants, and also performed the dances of the Playboy and the Shaman set to folk music with shamanistic rhythms.

Two Horsemen, dressed in white pantaloons and long white sleeveless coats over red jackets that were tied with yellow belts, and wearing red masks, came out from either side of the stage. Their hands covering their masks, they ran to the center of the stage, where they collided. Feigning surprise, they glanced at one another, turned around, and ran off in opposite directions. They swiftly went round the theater and then back to center stage where, spying one another, they feigned surprise again, turned, and ran off. They repeated this three or four times and at last danced, backstepping to folk music known as *Dodori Taryeong*, which included shamanistic rhythms. Finally a Buddhist Monk dressed in a robe of raw hemp that was tied with a hemp belt, and wearing hemp slippers, came running to center stage.

"*Hekkara! Hekkara!* Stand clear! Stand Clear!"

At last, the show was on. Prior to this, a procession, consisting of a Horseman at the head, followed by the Lion, the Monkey, the Buddhist Monk, a Head Monk, an Old Master Monk, the Young Shaman, Chwibari the Drunkard, a Nobleman, an Elderly Gentleman, and a Grandmother, made its way through the town. The musicians followed with their instruments. When they arrived at the place where they were to dance, they performed a small offertory, the Ceremony of the Masks.

The Mask Dance that began that evening did not finish until early dawn, when a small bonfire was built. For three nights, the town indulged in riotous merriment. These were nights when each moment was precious because of the excitement arising from the energetic dancing of the farmers' music troupe, the tightrope walking, the spinning of sieve wheels, and the tumbling of acrobats.

He could not possibly have imagined that Geum-ok's life would come to an end that May. Since then, May had become a month to shun and dislike. His favorite month had now become disagreeable. As the years passed, his health suffered, as though he were afflicted with an incurable disease that only the most violent poison could cure. The first few of these years were truly unbearable. Ever since this unavoidable separation in their childhood, he had often dreamed of her and wanted, on occasion, to see her, but he had never thought that he would miss her so desperately with the passing of time.

"Hey, why not get our kids together and become in-laws, huh?"

Whenever his father said this during his youth, her father would just drop his jaw with pleasure.

"What's the hurry? Expecting tea straight from the well?

"Aren't you going to wait for the persimmon to drop?" Bantering thus, with huge grins, they were happy. Her father's beard had the effect of enhancing his happiness when he was happy and his sadness when he was sad. His beard was so thick that when his daughter walked next to him, she looked like a little girl following an oak. She would never have looked this way, even if she had stood beside a real oak up on the mountain behind Shin-gwangsa Temple. An oak does not grow a beard and certainly does not grin like a catfish.

In his youth, he had not understood what the two fathers meant about becoming in-laws. As he got older, it began to dawn on him, even if only vaguely. No one told him anything, but he began to get the drift of it somewhat in the way the eggs of a salamander grow more distinctive day by day.

But her father was never to become an in-law to his father. One day, her father fell ill with cholera and never recovered. By the time his father had run to his side, he was already drawing his last breath, his face pale and speechless. He would no longer be like an oak leading his daughter, she looking like the little daughter of a mountain guardian. Her father was gone, just like that.

"I hope you will look after my daughter, Geum-ok. Please. Goodness, what miserable luck!"

Except for things of this nature which she conveyed to us, her mother could say nothing else. Her eyes were as red as holly-berries. It was hard to tell whether this was because of her crying so much or because of a growing animosity. The only thing his father could do for them was to draw the face of a man wearing a strange kind of headgear and have it hung above the doorway in their tumbledown, thatch-roofed cottage.

"Evil spirits bringing disease and other horrors will never again come near your house."

His father had been a comfort to her mother as he looked around the house, where the atmosphere was already tinged with a chill. What he had painted was a likeness of Cheo-yong. He had done this to prevent any more bad luck from striking the surviving mother and daughter. Her mother, who sat below the picture of Cheo-yong as if lost, may have gotten some comfort from it; but Geum-ok herself seemed even more afraid and tried to avoid it by looking off, her eyes large and hollow. While his father had worked away on it, she had hung around the house crying her eyes out.

"We should put one up in our house, too," his father said bluntly.

With her father's passing, there was no possibility now of their becoming in-laws, as they had so happily looked forward to. Everything seemed frustrating and mysterious, but there was nothing he could do to find out what the future held for himself and Geum-ok. Her father's passing made their promise, which had been ripening along with their laughter, now seem like a lizard that had given them the slip, leaving behind the stub of his tail. His father never brought up the subject again. And there was no way he could remind him about it.

But his father's efforts to save Geum-ok and her mother from disaster and disease were all in vain. In fact, what he once used to feel when he visited their house was only an ill-omen. What he later heard in their regard was all bad. The more misfortune became rampant, the fainter and more useless his reliance on the protection of Cheo-yong became. As faint, in fact, as Cheo-yong's face. There was nothing of use that her father had left them. All there was were some nets for trapping wild pheasants, badgers, and even blue marlin. But to his survivors, Geumok and her mother, they were of no use. Her father, who had been an expert in using nets, might have wanted to use them to trap her mother. But maybe his nets had instead trapped the Cheo-yong that my father had painted and that's why Cheo-yong was powerless. This probably explains why her mother went off with a migrant entertainer even before her mourning period was over. Some have said in defense of her that she went into the mountains because she had been possessed by spirits. But everyone knew that that was not true. Her mother had been completely taken with an acrobat, a dish-spinner who could spin circularrimmed strainers like no other, and even Cheo-yong had no power to stop her, perhaps because he, Cheo-yong, had been caught and entangled in a net.

His father had a bad taste in his mouth about this for a long time, even though he understood that times were hard and that it would only be a matter of minutes before some family would fall apart after being hit by some disaster. It did not take long for Geum-ok to be sent to a *gisaeng* house. She left home to become a *gisaeng*. Later, she went back home, the home everyone had left, scattering in all directions, in order to verify and confirm that everything had indeed happened. He felt that, if only the bearded man, her father, would appear again with his big bounding steps and suggest that they become in-laws, everything would go back to what it had been in the past and be intact. Nothing is so blind and immoral as what disappears.

♥

Time flowed on, but the image of Geum-ok would not leave him. His pain did not shrink. It only grew larger, like a knot on a tree. This was not just because of the half-baked promise their parents had made to each other, but because of something more primeval. If it is true that occasionally a man and a woman become attracted to each other for unknown reasons and become ill in mind and body, it must be the effect of ghostly spirits that spread diseases and the like.

Furthermore, whenever people talked about her physical beauty or skill as a dancer, he felt a sharp pain, as if an invisible thorn had pricked him in the heart. But when she was awarded a jade medal by the government for having attained the status of Distinguished *Gisaeng*, his suffering reached a peak. He thought he had been keeping it under control by resigning himself to it, but this had only been temporary.

♥

The twilight at dawn was a faint white. He had been hiding in an empty house and could not keep his troubled mind under control. There were not even any rats whose gnawing he could listen to. Just then, he felt a stinging in his toe. He examined it carefully. In the pale twilight, he could see a small cut that he had noticed long ago. He thought a mouse had bitten him. He thought he had heard mice in his sleep as he dreamt about his father and Cheo-yong by turns. A mouse must have gotten at his toe and bitten it. When he had first felt it being pricked, he had just ignored it, believing that a mouse would never dare bite a human being. But now the cut on the little toe of his right foot had stopped bleeding and had swollen up. Obviously, a mouse had bitten him. He went over in his mind what had happened when the mice were hopping about, raising a ruckus. But he was not sure when he had been bitten. It must have happened when his mind was elsewhere. Although the whole thing was unpleasant, the wound was nothing to worry about.

Where should he go?

The odor of the stable invaded his nostrils along with the fresh air of the morning. The stable must have been long abandoned. The hay on the floor was rotted and white with fungus, and the walls in places had mud missing, revealing stained cornstalks that looked like the ribs of a dog.

He finally decided to go look for Geum-ok. This had occurred to him while he was examining his mouse bite. He had missed her for a good long time. After the governor's office was closed and all government *gisaeng* let go, he had heard merely that she had gone to Gangnyeong. But he had never had the courage to go look for her. His little mouse bite saddened him very much, and somehow this made him determined to go look for her. It was hard to say whether or not she would recognize him. And even if she did recognize him, he could not expect to rely on her. Just as a drowning person might try to grab hold of a straw, he was reaching for an illusion of redemption by simply dreaming of her lovely face and figure. It was such a surprise to him that the great divide that existed between them could be so quickly filled by the sadness brought on by a small wound. He could not remain there a moment longer once he had made up his mind.

He took the mountain road and walked quickly. As the sun rose looking like a small drum, he quickened his steps. He did not think of himself as a fugitive. He was going back to his old home. Even though he was on a path that was a shortcut through the mountains, he kept thinking he was taking the long way there. And he was hungry—but he was in a hurry.

More than likely, there had been a huge uproar when the bodies of his younger sister and that bastard were discovered.

He thought of telling Geum-ok everything, and then putting everything else off until the next question had to be decided. Until he got to her and confided everything to her, there were only a few hours of reprieve.

Climbing on a wild cherry tree, the shoot of an arrowroot reached out into the air. Birds were hopping about under the young pines. As he walked along at a strong pace, he felt as if he had been walking like this for several decades, or even for several centuries. The oaks held their old brown leaves from the previous year and would do so until late spring. He thought of the hooting of the owls of the night before. By the time the daylight was gone and the owls started hooting, he would have to see her. At least by the time the owls started hooting….

A good part of the day was over. The road led in to the fields. The barley had all been harvested, and the wet fields were busily being combed with rakes. No one would ever recognize him. But he kept a sharp lookout anyway.

"So where are you headed?"

When one of the pair of elderly traveling companions who appeared to be peasants asked him this as he encountered them on the road, he answered with some off-the-wall remark: The Gangnyeong Mask Dance seems to have lost it.

"You must be going to Gangnyeong."

"I was thinking of stopping by."

"Then you should head for Bongsan or Girin. The Gangnyeong Mask Dance is quite tame, right from the start."

"Of course. It's a dance for the middle class."

The two elderly men looked at each other and nodded in agreement. They must have already had a drink, as their faces were red, like the mask of the Horseman.

"Well, yes. Bongsan and Girin are terrific, all right. But I've already been there, so …"

He took pains to make sure that the elderly gentlemen would not pay any great heed to him. Luckily, they didn't seem to sense anything out of the ordinary. He was inwardly hoping that he might hear some news of Geum-ok from some of their offhand remarks.

"I never made it to the top as Boss, but I was right under him, playing the role of Pockmarked Puss, and I toured the whole country…." The man carrying the sickle with the handle wrapped with a straw rope was mumbling, his gaze set afar, as he reminisced on the old days:

"Oh, yeah … yeah…. Keep going, man!" The other gentleman interjected in the dialogue-style of the Mask Dance, and his comment seemed to be teasing him with its hint of "uh-oh, there you go again!"

He chimed in to flatter the man with the sickle: "You must have had fun."

"Sure! Can't tell you how much fun it was. I've seen the Lion Dance of Hamgyeong-do Province, the Old Fox Dance of Jolla-do Province, the Playboy Dance of Seoul, and the Mask Dance of Gyeongsang-do Province. But nothing comes close to our dance in Hwanghae-do Province. I tell you, nothing at all."

When he had finished talking, the elderly man suddenly lifted his right foot, raised his right hand to form a straight line with his left hand; then, breaking form as he bent at the waist and knees, he seemed to be about to soar off into the sky. Finally, he leaped nimbly, shook his face, and made a half-turn to the side. Then he lifted his other foot and set it down, moving it to the opposite side.

"Isn't this our basic movement?"

"It's close to the Bongsan style."

They really seemed to be enjoying themselves.

"It's because the Bongsan style is exuberant. But the dance has to move from one dance to two and then from two sets to double sets twice in order to get its true flavor." The gentleman who had demonstrated his dance said this with a bit of nostalgia and began to quicken the pace of the trip.

The young man was suffering not only from hunger, but also from the aching in all his joints and muscles, which was brought on by the long walk. It was difficult for him to endure the occasional stinging in his toes. But he managed to walk along with them without showing any sign of it. It was safer for him to travel with his companions than to do it alone without anyone.

There was silence for a long while. Cuckoos were crying out on the mountain across from the road they were on.

"Now, the Gangnyeong dance will probably get much better. I heard that the Gwangchol-li Group also gets together every night to learn from Geum-ok."

"Did I hear you say Geum-ok?"

"Yes. You know, the Geum-ok who was bestowed a jade medal by the King."

A thunderbolt hit him. The gentleman, the dancer, knew of her. He swallowed. Realizing that he had reached the point he had been waiting for, he grew anxious.

"Does this woman, Geum-ok, teach dance?"

The only thing he knew was that she had gone to Gangnyeong. He certainly did not want to miss anything that might be said about her.

"Not just dance. She is such an outstanding singer and dancer."

The gentleman who was the dancer answered with pride, as if it were enough for him just to have heard of her.

"Really!"

"If you go to Gangnyeong, you'd better go to Galmoro to see Geumok."

"Galmoro?"

"Yeah, it's just across the bridge from Gangnyeong."

The word Galmoro landed deeper in his heart than any of the other words. "I will get to Galmoro before the owls begin hooting." Then he remembered the two pictures of Cheo-yong that his father had painted and hung up. If his fate had brought him on such a roundabout way to see her again, the paintings of Cheo-yong must have provided the two of them with special spiritual powers that protected them. After the government office of Haeju had closed, Geum-ok had settled in Galmoro, Gangnyeong, and devoted her life to teaching song and dance to talented performers. When he arrived in Galmoro, the owls were about to begin their hooting.

It was again the season when the owls would be hooting. In every performance of the Mask Dance, there would always be a Monk wearing a mask and hat, a long hemp robe tied with an arrowroot belt, and hemp sandals, who would dash out into the center and shout:

"*Hekkara! Hekkara!* Stand clear! Stand clear!"

A small bonfire would illuminate his mask, which was not any different than those of other Monks. No one would know who he was....

♥

I was so obsessed with who the real Geum-ok was, and with her sad history in the development of the Mask Dance, that I forgot my girlfriend was next to me. I started shouting *"Hekkara! Hekkara!"* as if I had become someone who had to play the role of the Monk through some twist of an ill-fated life.

"Oh, no. What is it this time?"

My girlfriend had awakened and was looking at me suspiciously, as if I had gone off the deep end. But I was speechless, though I may have had a twinkle of pride in my eye from having been looking into the traditional culture of the land where I belong, namely Korea. Even if I were to try talking to her seriously, it was questionable whether, in her sleepiness, she would care to know what I had been up to: signaling the beginning of a Mask Dance with a shout, or going off the deep end.

♥

About the time I was intent on tracing the footsteps of the Lion, a mummy was discovered in the ancient city of Loulan, in the Western Region. When my friend saw the newspaper article about it, sure as could be, he got excited: "A mummy! What a fantastic story!" I put a wet blanket on it at once. What does a Chinese mummy have to do with us? was my main point.

"Why do you get so worked up about a mummy? You keep saying, mummy, mummy. What the heck does a mummy have to do with anything?" I shot back.

Nevertheless, I felt that there was some thread of extraordinary cause-and-effect, in view of the fact that the Lion I was pursuing went back to the Silla Dynasty and, even farther, to the West of China. The reason I could never confide in him about this was because I was afraid he might try to make a premature "dramatization" of it. He was already talking about "The Mummy Awakens." My inspiration was simple: a Silla Lion, traveling in the desert, meets a man who has been asleep for a thousand years. Guided by this premise, I read article after article about the mummy, day after day. Loulan was in ruins, at the eastern end of the Tarim Basin. That basin is the delta of the Tarim River, which flows into Wandering Lake, Lop Nur. Because of the desert, the river changes course frequently, and Wandering Lake moves as well. During the Wei Dynasty, Loulan, which was one of the many city states of the Western Region, became a ruin largely through the forces of nature.

The heyday of Loulan was, at the latest, around A.D. 330, and when the houses, temples, and tombs were excavated, many archaeological objects were found which showed the influence of Gandhara civilization, and, as with the woven metal, the Roman. In addition, there were bronze mirrors, bronze arrowheads, earthenware, and patterned silk, all in the Chinese-style of the Han Dynasty. It was in these desert ruins that a mummy, in "excellent condition," was discovered. It was called "The Girl of Loulan," and according to the newspapers, her clothes were so intact that they would be great for the study of the costumes of that time. Unlike the Egyptian mummies, which were dehydrated by artificial means, "The Girl of Loulan" was mummified naturally because of the dry climate and desert soil. Anyhow, because I had dumped on him right from the start, he could not manage to bring up the subject of "the mummy" (meaning, "The Girl of Loulan") again.

♥

Only when there was a short time left before I had to meet my girlfriend did he dismiss "the kids." The whole time I had been thinking about the sad Lion that was going back and forth with the Monk, and about the lion in the mural of the Dunhuang cave. Nothing special occurred to me in regards to the lion of the West when I heard about "The Girl of Loulan" being excavated, or when I saw the murals of the Dunhuang cave. But after having watched the video, I don't know by what sort of providence, I suddenly thought of a connection with the mural of the Dunhuang cave. But I never mentioned a word of it to him, even when we found ourselves alone.

"The kids who say they want to carry on our culture don't seem to understand our music and what's in our bones...."

Dragging his chair over so he could sit by me, he talked to himself with some solemnity.

"What do you mean, 'bones'?"

"I mean, the body. The movement of the body. Dance."

I kept quiet. Then he said, "We must have drunk a lot last night." He shook his head.

"That's all because of your *hyangga*."

I smiled faintly as I thought of all my embarrassing behavior of the night before. He smiled, too, even though he had no idea why.

"Anyway, what is this about your girlfriend running away? I can kind of understand it, since you've been unemployed for a year-and-a-half."

He looked at me as if to say, "She couldn't have!"

"A woman running away from home can be a beautiful thing, right?" I went off on a tangent. "I want you to work on the play about Dunhuang, or Don Juan, the Playboy, by yourself. I can't even think about it." I was making an excuse for myself.

"Why? Because of your girlfriend?"

"Hey, you're the one who asked about my girlfriend running away. And you're out of work too, aren't you? What the hell are you picking on me for, when we're in the same line of business?"

He snickered when I said, "the same line of business.".

"Then why don't we work together since we're in this same line of business. Let's form a company or, rather, a theater group. Heck, we already have an office. What's keeping us from forming one? Theater Group the 'Two-Horned Beast.' You have one horn and I have the other, so that makes us two-horned. But we have one body. How about that?"

"Don't be ridiculous. How can we become one body? Are you out of your gourd?"

"Let's not worry about that now. But how about the 'Two-Horned Beast'?"

"There's nothing special about a 'Two-Horned Beast.' Have you ever seen a horned animal not having two horns?"

"A rhinoceros."

"A rhinoceros? Rhinos have two horns—one in front and one in the back—that are formed through the accumulation of keratin.

"Then what does 'unicorn' mean?"

"I see you picked that up somewhere."

Whether he was listening or not, he kept on snickering. Having been frivolous long enough, he straightened up and lit a cigarette.

"I'm going to tell you something as a co-representative of the Two-Horned Beast. I heard something new not long ago. An astonishing story."

I just sneered.

"It's about the stuff found at Dunhuang. Remember what the Japanese guy, Ōtani, took?"

He seemed to be checking to see whether I knew about that part of the story or not, so I nodded and said there had been a Japanese party among the plunderers.

"Right. You've been looking into it. Good. Some of that stuff is supposed to be in our country."

He lowered his voice.

"The stuff from Dunhuang?" I was really surprised. "Where is it?"

"In the basement of the National Museum."

He obviously felt good about this.

"Why would it be there?"

"How would I know? They say it's been there since the Japanese occupation."

He added that he had checked with several "knowledgeable sources."

I did not know how to take this. Although I knew he liked to collect far-out stories, I believed he would never tell lies of this kind. All I could do was tilt my head. I didn't get it. The expeditions deserved to be censured for having taken things out after having bribed the head monk. And the execution of the head monk was also understandable. But what should we make of the fact that the objects that had been taken away by the Japanese were in our country? Even before it crossed my mind that history can sometimes be totally bizarre, I realized that there had to be something unusual behind it. I was getting mixed up. To be glad that these objects were in our country would be childish. Because it would mean that the objects were being squandered somewhere here in Korea. Wouldn't that make us accomplices of the crime the Japanese committed? One could see how a great power such as Great Britain would display its loot in the British Museum as a matter of pride; no matter how such things got into our country, it was still something we should congratulate ourselves about—we should consider our country's interests first and foremost; and this was even more so the case in regard to our own culture—all these thoughts assailed me.

But for all this confusion, I have to admit that Hyecho, who had been a vague and unknowable character to me, suddenly felt like someone I was very close to.

It was because of this that, as I hurriedly took my leave from him so as to meet my girlfriend on time, I resolved to dig a little deeper into "The Love of Dunhuang." Even if I didn't feel confident enough to attempt a dramatization of the story, I thought that it would be worth looking into. More precisely, I was not worried about what he was thinking of in regard to "The Love of Dunhuang". I thought of Hyecho's performance of the Lion Dance and about the Lion, the King of Beasts, dancing as if he wanted to fly, but really concealing the truth of his loneliness inside the Lion—the soul behind this lonely face had been transferred to a painting on a wall and finally returned home after a millennium plus a few more hundred years. The San-ye of Silla was known to have originated in the West and therefore it seemed natural to assume that Hyecho must have encountered the Lion Dance in his travels. Having gotten this far, I felt as though I had been anxious to see the caves and their murals long before my friend started to tell me about Dunhuang, the Mogao Caves, and Hyecho.

The region west of China. I had my own memory of it myself. My relationship with that region may not have been direct, but it was how I experienced the strange world that is to the west of China.

♥

I was working for a weekly magazine. Whenever I think of that time, I can still hear a certain young girl's singing. It wasn't great singing. Her voice trembled delicately, a very young and untrained voice. Shall I say that I detected fragility in her voice, which obviously had not been much used? I was certainly aware of a sadness about her. Because she did not sing very well, she made the listener somewhat nervous about it. She must have been worried that she might make a mistake. Of course, this had to do with pitch. One could probably talk about tonic, dominant, or subdominant chords as in western music, but with her kind of singing, there was no right or wrong way. For no one knew what the original condition of the song was. A song that is left with only the lyrics and no music is, in a way, dead. Anyhow, I kept hoping she would not make even one mistake. I suppose this doesn't make much sense. Weren't the songs she was singing much more ancient than the music we sing, which is structured according to a full tonal system? It might have had a melody that only a few people would have sung. So there is no reason to speak of the twelve major and minor tones, or the five tones: *Gung*, *Sang*, *Gak*, *Chi*, and *Wu*. I repeat: songs that have been left to us with only the lyrics and no tune are like a body without a soul. Or, they are more like tarnished bones or the skeleton of an old corpse, the flesh of which has all decomposed. Strangely enough, I keep hearing her singing in my head.

The girl joined her hands in front of her, took a deep breath, and opened her mouth. What was she going to sing? We listened. She told us that it would be a song her grandfather had taught her. So I was expecting to hear a folk song from Hamgyeong-do Province, as that was where her grandfather was from. I was expecting either the lilting "Shingosan Taryeong" or "Lamentations of Hamgyeong-do Province." But I was wrong. She was a little tense and made nervous by the fact that she was performing before an audience, but she was not awkward. Her cheeks were flushed, and as she started to sing, her voice trembled. She resembled an amateur playing a reed instrument. But that lasted only a short while. She recovered and held to the pitch. But on the whole it trembled delicately.

When she started singing, I nearly burst out laughing. She was quite natural, but I felt there was something awkward about her. It might have been because she stood as a real professional singer might stand. But just as I was on the verge of laughing, I realized that she might end up not being able to sing. So I stifled my laughter. It was also true that I had no reason to listen to her. I only wanted to listen to her because I had a little time. I have a habit of not looking at any person I talk with, and so watching someone sing was such a novel experience that I actually broke out in a sweat. But because she was so young, I managed to look her way several times without feeling too uncomfortable. A small kerchief tied around her head, her round face seemed perched on her lime-green blouse. Her cheeks were flushed the clear red of a silk tree blossom, and on her nose, beads of sweat had formed. Every time she opened her mouth, I saw the tip of her tongue, red between neat rows of teeth.

I glanced at Jo, our news photographer, at the time. He looked a little confused. He appeared to want to go right back to the office or to go somewhere for a drink. He was a news photographer, and I had been working with him for such a long time on assignments that we got along pretty well. But I was the one who wanted to hear the girl sing. Jo had no interest in it.

Actually, I wasn't at ease enough to listen to her either. The weekly that I was working for at the time had "not much going for it," as the saying went. First of all, the magazine did not have a clear focus. It seemed reasonable enough that it dealt with culture and entertainment, but to deal with a doctoral thesis and how much entertainers make in the same magazine seemed incongruous. Even though we didn't have much going, the amount of work that occupied us was second to none. The finances of management, which had jumped into the business thinking there were a lot of important things going on, were quite weak, and management was unable to hire the people that were needed and was barely able to fill in the gaps with existing workers. So our work was much greater, and we were busier than those who worked for other, better weeklies which had "something going for them." In addition, the reporters needed to have professional knowledge in many fields, as their articles had to be longer than those of the daily papers.

The subject of the so-called need to train specialist reporters came up. It was true that we needed to do this. No one would argue against a professional literary reporter reporting on literature, a professional reporter for publications writing on publications, a reporter specializing in drama reporting on drama, etc. It would have been the right thing to do. But there was a real shortage of manpower. The situation was such that one person assumed, not just two roles, but three or even four. At every meeting, the subject of specialist reporters came up again and again, but it was impossible from the beginning. It wasn't that we had not identified fields of specialization according to some principles. But after a week or two, the push would just dissipate. There was also the issue of whether or not the categories were too diverse.

So, week after week, we reporters were just running every which way, regardless of our abilities. I had often heard monthly magazine workers say they had no idea how the time passed, and indeed I felt this to be true in my case, too. We had to do everything—from planning, making contacts, and covering the stories, to doing the writing, and then proofreading just before the magazine went to the printer. Because this process was repeated week after week, we had to move like cogs on a wheel, every day, without ever stopping. We were short of manpower and short of time. Forget specialization. One became a specialist the same week one took on an assignment.

The project I was in charge of was called "Terminal Sites." Projects of the weeklies tended to be rehashes of old ideas that had been around for a long time, with the format changed slightly. This was especially the case when there was no manpower to mobilize. Everyone complained that we should rid ourselves of our complacency, but it was no use. We just kept at it, filling up blank pages. The ideas for "Terminal Sites" must have been planned in the same way, somewhere, sometime ago. But we decided to go ahead with it, consoling ourselves with the thought that it was the first of its kind. As the word "terminal" suggests, it was a project which focused on old things that were disappearing, one by one, in our generation. Because the times were changing so quickly, many things were becoming remote and disappearing. We didn't have to mull over "terminal" too long. By way of illustration: The small fine-tooth combs and the hairpins that our grandmothers used to use or the horsehair hats that our grandfathers used to wear were subjects of our reporting. We were not limited just to objects of daily use. We also covered eunuchs and court ladies, whose duties were unique in the old dynastic period and who would never again play any role in our society; and also disappearing customs. With regard to customs, there was a great variety of them, ranging from children's kite-flying to the poetry gatherings of country elders. The houses with oak-shingle roofs known as *neowajip* in mountain villages where slash-and-burn farmers lived provided a "terrific story." The shingles were made from oak that had been cut and sawn into planks and then laid on the roof like tiles. When we went to Gang-won-do Province, Jo was beside himself at seeing these mountain people watching TV in their homes, and he took lots of pictures with his camera.

Our special reports on "Terminal Sites" gradually began to lose steam after the feature went past number fifteen. Our project had begun with quite a bit of enthusiasm following a wave of Korean studies in numerous fields. Prior to the beginning of the series, we went far and wide to gather material, and we made notes on future sources; but it was not an easy job to produce a feature article every week. Since "Terminal Sites" implied that something was disappearing, it was no easy matter to find the sites themselves. Our meager stipends, no bigger than a mouse's tail, did not help our pace.

Above all, there was the problem of inertia. Jo must have felt the same way, as he would perfunctorily ask, "What is it this week?" only when we were about to go out to work on the story. The only thing that ever got us excited was our coverage of the *neowajip*, the houses with the oak-shingle roofs in Gang-won-do Province. We were quite happy and proud to have spent a few nights in a valley deep in the mountains, drinking *makkeoli* and eating *dotori muk* [an acorn starch gelatin]. But these kinds of shallow pleasures, though very elegant, did not last long. I thought it probably best to extend the project a few more times and finish the series after the twentieth feature.

Even though our weekly didn't have much going for it, a variety of stories came to us through many different kinds of people from every level of society. They all wanted us to write their stories, but most of it was junk. There were hints of unheard-of ideologies, of some award being given to the wrong person, or of some new discovery, etc. Flyers for events and information on news items piled up like trash if we left them unexamined for a day. We came to realize what "flood of information" meant. From this vantage point, it was exciting to deal, in depth, with what was substantive in life, and what was not.

♥

It was a day in May. "Terminal Sites" would discontinue in two or three installments. Because we had started the series as a special feature for the new year and had four installments a month, by the end of May we would have completed twenty installments. One day, I heard from my friend that he had someone in mind as a subject for "Terminal Sites." He told me that he had met this old man entirely by accident, while drinking *makkeoli* at a mineral-water spring.

"Does *makkeoli* gush from the ground in your neck of the woods?"

I was not at all interested in the story. I already had two or three other stories in mind to fill the column.

"There's a place right next to the spring. You know, their liquor tastes pretty good there."

I knew that there was a little mineral-water spring in back of the neighborhood where he lived. According to my friend, the old man started showing up in the early spring, and there was something about him that gave him a certain air. My friend frequented the mineral-water spring whenever he had a chance, and often bumped into the old fellow.

They finally had a drink together. The old man had recently moved into the neighborhood, across from my friend's place. The houses in the neighborhood were all shacks. My friend found out later that the old man lived with distant relatives. But he and the old man became close, and they talked about one thing and another. One day he heard a story that he could not fathom. My friend, of course, knew that I was searching for stories for "Terminal Sites" and knew vaguely what the column was about. Talk about "being vague": There wasn't much difference between us on that score.

"You know what *gonghu* is, don't you?"

My friend asked me this after telling me a long story about the old man.

"Kung Fu? The Chinese martial art?"

I was reminded of the Kung Fu sign I saw occasionally, in the third-floor window of a building somewhere. It was spelled KUNGFU and I thought it should have been spelled as Kungpu, as "f" is generally spelled with a "p" in Korean. Such useless things were going through my mind. This is probably the sorry plight of those who eke out a living minding the niceties of their language.

"Not that. It's *gonghu, gonghu.*

"*Gonghu*?"

I suddenly thought of aristocratic titles, like Duke, Earl, Count, Viscount, and Baron, as the first two letters of Duke and Earl in Korean made the acronym *gong-hu*. But just then I decided that he might be talking about the ancient musical instrument, the *gonghu*.

"I mean the musical instrument—the *gonghu*."

When he actually said, "musical instrument," I was a little dumbfounded. He and I had never talked about musical instruments. On top of that, the *gonghu* is an ancient instrument that not much is known about and is nowhere to be found. After he said "musical instrument," I pretended that, of course, I was familiar with it. But, actually, all I knew was that it was a stringed instrument. I had no idea what it even looked like. The reason I was able to pretend that I knew what it was, was that I vaguely recalled having read, somewhere in a high school textbook, of a song known as *Gonghu-in*. Together with *Song of the Oriol* ... wasn't *Gonghu-in* one of the oldest songs of Korea?

Anyway, it was unexpected. But even then I was made mildly curious by the sheer fact that he would even mention a classical instrument. But when I heard the ensuing story, it occurred to me that it might really make an article for the magazine. According to my friend, the old man, whom he thought had such an unusual air about him, had worked all over

Manchuria as a migrant worker, and had played the *gonghu* because he loved musical instruments. So that was the connection between the old man and the *gonghu*. My friend didn't think much of it when he learned what the old man did; but when he got home and searched through his books, he discovered that there was no one who knew how to play the *gonghu* anymore.

"Isn't that surprising? That makes him the last person known to play the *gonghu*. Shouldn't I get some kind of treat for reporting this story to you?"

He was being flippant.

"Treat? Even if it's true, there's nothing about it that would appeal to the public. Kung Fu might be more appealing, but it's Chinese...."

Since I had so little confidence in regard to the *gonghu*, I had hedged a bit. To be sure, I thought it might make a good final installment for "Terminal Sites". Although I was very unfamiliar with the *gonghu*, at least it seemed worth writing about. If, indeed, the old man was the only surviving person who could play the instrument, precisely as my friend had said, it would be a perfect end-piece to the series of twenty features.

Of course, I couldn't accept everything my friend told me. I knew that he was interested in what I was doing and wanted to help, but he was an outsider when it came to my job. It's not that he was untrustworthy. He actually made it harder because he was too serious. But I couldn't just hop aboard. However humble our weekly publication was, the articles had to be justified and valid. I started to do a little research into the *gonghu*, to verify what my friend had told me. Even if only superficially, I had to make myself a professional reporter—an expert on the *gonghu*.

I looked through a few books in our reference room and then made a phone call to the National Academy of Classical Music. What sort of musical instrument was the *gonghu*, and what status did it have now? But it wasn't easy to find out. To begin with, there were several kinds of *gonghu*. There was a variety of models: an upright *gonghu* called the *su-gonghu*; a flat *gonghu* called the *wa-gonghu*; a *bongsu-gonghu* with legs and the head of a phoenix; a large *gonghu* called the *dae-gonghu*; and a small one called the *so-gonghu*.

Furthermore, different books listed different models. Although they were all listed as *gonghu*, the difference between them seemed greater than that between the *geo-mun-go* and the *gayageum*. One thing common among the *gonghu* was that they were all originally from the region to the west of China. They were also used in China and Japan, and in Korea during the Goguryeo and Baekje periods. The Western harp also originated from this instrument. The number of strings is an important characteristic of string instruments. The *geo-mun-go* has six strings and the *gayageum* has twelve. But the *gonghu* has been recorded as having different numbers of strings, according to different books.

The upright model had either 21 or 23 strings; the number of strings for a flat model ranged from 4 to 21, and the phoenix-head *gonghu* had 20 strings. I couldn't make heads or tails of this instrument. For someone like me who had only played a harmonica, it was difficult even to write an introductory note, let alone the report of an expert. In this regard, it was obvious that I would have a lot of trouble writing an article, if I decided to do so. The circumstances of exactly when and how the instrument had been introduced were unclear, except for the fact that it came from the West. There was not even any mention of it in the old records. The only mention of it comes in a Chinese historical book entitled *Sooseo* (Book of the Sui Dynasty) where it says the *gonghu* was played in Goguryeo and Baekje. I felt pretty lost. I was never sure what the instrument was. And no one knows how it was played either, because there is no record on the subject.

My interest grew in proportion to my ignorance of it. When my friend talked to me about it, I just thought it might do *something* for us, but instead I found myself being dragged into the dark and mysterious world of the instrument. I was living as if time were moving like cogs on a wheel. I spent several days searching through a number of books. But I found nothing. I did, however, discover that the *gonghu* which is currently preserved in Korea was purchased in Beijing in 1937 by a certain Ham Hwajin, who was a master conductor of *A-ak*, the classical court music. I could make no more progress than that. My desire to delve into this matter, which was as meager as the company's fee for the report, naturally dwindled.

♥

The last column of "Terminal Sites" was supposed to be on the funeral bier. It was only about two or three decades ago that it was not uncommon to see a bier. I still vividly remember seeing a colorful one being carried off. A man at the front of the procession led the singing by calling out the prologue and ringing the cluster of small bells. Then the pallbearers would respond in song. I wanted to go visit the warehouses in the countryside where they were stored, and to write on the remaining biers and their paraphernalia. Then I was going to publish the lyrics of the songs they sang for a funeral procession at the beginning of the piece: *If you leave now, when will you return? Once you're gone, it's for good. Don't they say, Bukmang Mountain is far away? It's only a hop, skip, and a jump!*

If I hadn't received a phone call from my friend, I would have gone ahead with this plan. It happened in the afternoon of the very day I was thinking of going out into the field for the report the next day.

"So, what do you think of the *gonghu*? Why are you so mum about it?"

The moment he spoke, I felt I was being aroused suddenly from a deep sleep. Something passed through my mind like lightning. At the same time, I was overwhelmed by the certainty that I had to write up something on the *gonghu*.

This story took place during the Ancient Joseon period. One morning, a man named Gwagnijago went down to the river to board a boat. A white-haired old man appeared and drowned in the river. His wife came after him, playing the *gonghu* and singing mournfully. She also drowned in the river. Gwagnijago, who had witnessed the tragedy, returned home and told his wife, Yeo-ok, what he had seen. Thus saddened, Yeo-ok composed and sang a dirge in the dead wife's stead. This was the dirge, in fact, called the *Gonghu-in*. I started taking detailed notes from the *Gonghu-in*. I could not figure out why I suddenly felt impelled to work on the *gonghu* instead of on the biers. But that impulse took hold of me and became a conviction. I even found out from my friend where our old man lived. His house was nearest to the mineral-water spring and should be easy to find. I searched all afternoon to find out what sort of instrument the *gonghu* was. But nothing clear seemed to emerge, however intense about it I was.

It was by complete coincidence that I discovered a photograph of the bronze bell in Sang-wonsa Buddhist Temple. I had seen several such designs on temple bells before. They were images of *heavenly winged beings*. A *heavenly lady* would be flying sideways at a slight angle in heaven, her garment fluttering. The musical instrument she would be holding in her arms was none other than the *gonghu*.

The moment I saw this image of the *heavenly lady* in the design of the bell, I muttered to myself, "Aha, this is it!" Out of a completely dense fog, I began to see light. I am not saying that the image of the *heavenly lady* holding the *gonghu* in her arms was anything out of the ordinary. I happened to have seen this image several times in the past, without taking any special notice of it, while I was at work on some historical materials. Frankly, I hadn't known that the instrument she was holding was a *gonghu.* To me, it had been nothing more than a decoration showing a *winged-being* flying sideways, sculpted in relief on a bell. But when I recognized that the instrument she was holding was the *gonghu*, I felt that I was watching a *heavenly lady* descending from heaven, to the mysterious and exquisite sounds of the *gonghu*. It was no longer just a decoration on a bell. I felt I could hear the ringing of the bell in the sky, as if it were an echo chamber. She was a true *living angel.* She was an *angel*, alive and breathing. Although I was quite aware that I might be dreaming, my heart throbbed and I was flush, as if meeting a woman clandestinely.

The next day, after lunch, we set out to look for the old man. I was all set to go, first thing in the morning, but Jo, the reporter with the photography department, was busy with other work, and so we had to put it off until the afternoon. Because the old man didn't have a phone, we had to rush over as soon as we could.

"Even though the old man may have played the *gonghu*, he may not have one, so why don't you just take some pictures of him?"

"That doesn't sound too good. Isn't there some way we can borrow a *gonghu*?"

It was understandable that a photographer would say this.

"I heard that the National Museum has one. Why don't you go borrow it?"

I was worried that we would not even be able to find the old man at home, let alone find an instrument. I was reminded of what my department chief used to tell us reporters when we were desperate to meet a deadline: "Imagine you're sitting under the typeset board while the papier-mâché mold is being made." In case I wasn't able to see the old man, to avoid being flattened by the typeset board, I had to have someone else to interview and get an article ready in one day. While on our way to the old man's house in a taxi, I was busy putting together the connections between the *Gonghu-in*, Yeo-ok's Dirge, and the *gonghu* held by the *flying angel* on the bronze temple bell. I thought that there had to be a connection if my article were to have any life. I was also anxious to make the sounds of the *gonghu* being played by the *angel* more alive and vivid.

Jo and I climbed the hill covered with shacks. My friend had told me that the old man had told him that I had permission to visit him any time. He had also said that the old man, quite unexpectedly for someone his age, had a twinkle in his eyes and became enthusiastic whenever the *gonghu* was mentioned. Still, I had some reservations. The *gonghu* seemed like an instrument for women rather than men. Yeo-ok was a woman and so was the *heavenly being* with her decorative drapings. There was no evidence that the *gonghu* had ever been played by a man. Even the harp, which can be considered a cousin to the *gonghu*, was only depicted as being played by women in Greek paintings. This, of course, did not prove that the *gonghu* had never been played by a man. Nevertheless, as we got closer to the old man's house, I began to sense the futility of it all. We were pretty certain that no one knew how to play the *gonghu*. Yet, here was this old man who said that he knew how to play one. Strictly speaking, this wasn't something to make light of. It could amount to a very special discovery. Thinking that the sudden decision to choose the *gonghu* for the last feature of our series might have been a kind of a revelation, I became serious, without letting on to Jo.

It wasn't as easy to find the old man's house as my friend had said it would be.

In spite of the fact that his house was supposed to be located opposite that of my friend, it was over a hill, and we were only looking in the vicinity of my friend's place. We asked every person we met along the way, but no one knew.

"Wow, this neighborhood is something else!"

In spite of his reputation as a master at finding houses thanks to the keen eye he had as a photographer, Jo was at a loss in this slum of cardboard shacks cramped tightly together.

"Wait a minute. Let's go have a shot of *makkeoli* later. I know a good place, next to the mineral-water spring. I heard that their liquor is out of this world."

"I'm already dying of thirst. I could drink buckets."

It was a muggy day in May. We had been climbing up and down the hill, and now our backs were drenched with sweat. I could tell that Jo was grumbling to himself, wondering why the hell we had to come to such a crummy neighborhood full of shacks: "Terminal Sites" was not this important. Jo and I were usually on good terms, but as soon as we teamed up to do a project together, he would become so pompous that I was left stupefied about photographers altogether.

It was past four o'clock when we finally found the old man's house. We had to look for it at the other end of the neighborhood where my friend lived. It was supposed to have been the house nearest to the mineral-water spring, but I didn't know that there was another narrow street that ran off in another direction. The house had a dark roof, just as my friend had told me.

"Right house?" Jo asked, as he wiped the sweat off his forehead.

"Absolutely. Look. The house in front has a collection of empty bottles."

We entered the narrow courtyard as I pointed to the pile of empty liquor bottles in one corner of it. There were no real gates or fences, so actually the courtyard was not even enclosed.

"Is anybody home?"

The doors were closed and there was no sign of anyone. I was beginning to wonder if I had been pinning too much on the piece of information my friend had provided.

"Hello? Anybody home?" I called out again.

If there were no one around, I would be crushed. If I had to go back without meeting the old man, I would be lost, and not a soul would have any sympathy for me. Fortunately, I heard something, as if someone were straightening out his clothing. Just as I was looking at Jo with an air of anticipation, the door of a room slowly opened.

"Who is it?"

I could not believe my eyes. Jo looked at me, also in complete surprise. It was not the old man who showed his face. It was a young girl who, at first glance, seemed maybe sixteen or seventeen. She came out of the room, but she was instinctively suspicious.

"The old gentleman is not at home, is he?"

I was suddenly anxious. At that moment, a faint shadow passed across her face. I knew something was wrong. I had meant to say "the old man who played the *gonghu,*" but I had checked myself. I didn't think the girl would know anything about the *gonghu*. She hesitated, blinking. To put her at ease, we introduced ourselves as reporters and explained that we had come to interview the old gentleman. I also asked, with a smile, what her relationship to him was.

"You mean my grandfather? He passed away some time ago." It was such a direct answer.

"Passed away?"

"He fell sick suddenly and lay down. He never got up again."

I felt my face harden. I knew one could never tell about the health of the elderly, but I could not believe that this was happening. Moreover, what was I going to do about the project? I thought I might have bee making a mistake when I had suddenly changed my plans because of a whim. And it should have spelled trouble when my friend made his suggestion out of the blue. It had been my fault to get sidetracked on something like the *gonghu*. Now our project had fallen to pieces. If only the old man were alive and could be photographed, we could patch together an article. But it was all over now. I could feel myself going limp. Now I would have to stay up all night tomorrow, to avoid getting put under the press. I could not turn away, just because I heard that the old man had died. Maybe I didn't care for the way the whole thing was turning out. Suddenly, I felt defiant, wanting very much to salvage something from our visit. I was not about to let everything I had gone through come to nothing, even if the old man was gone, and even if his story might have turned out to be only useless, idle talk about bygone days.

In fishing, don't they talk about the big one that got away? My regret at not being able to see the old man was just too much for me. I should have gone to find him immediately after my friend had told me about him. And he might have been a much more mysterious figure. Quite aside from "Terminal Sites," there were many precious old things that were disappearing without a trace in our time and from our society, just as certain species of animals were becoming extinct. The old man must have been one of them. But no one had noticed. How terrible! I became indignant and started to kick myself for how lackadaisical I had been about the whole matter.

"Don't we have to stay up all night?" Jo muttered at me. He meant we should leave. I nodded. But my regret was only growing. The images of Yeo-ok and the *flying angel* would not leave my head. Of course, the whole thing was useless. The *heavenly lady* on the temple bell had gotten stuck in solid metal as she was flying over to me.

"Miss, have you ever heard of the *gonghu*, by any chance?" I was reluctantly about to turn away when I asked her this. I wasn't expecting much. But she surprised me.

"Yes, I have. My grandfather told me about it."

I turned toward her, startled. What could the old man have told his granddaughter about the *gonghu*? I could hardly contain myself. Even if what she had to say were a dud for the magazine, I had to listen.

"So what did he tell you? This is why we're here: to hear what he had to say." I approached her, careful not to intimidate her. I thought she might actually give us some kind of clue. She seemed to hesitate a little, just as she had when she first came out of the room. However, she began to speak with ease. I concentrated on what she was saying. It didn't make sense that a girl of sixteen or seventeen was telling me about the *gonghu*. "There was a man living by the riverside...." I was soon disappointed. This was nothing more than what the old song, the *Gonghu-in*, said. The old man who relished telling his old stories must have told her this one, too. I listened until she was finished, even though I had the whole thing written down in my notebook already. Anyhow, the old man had been no ordinary man. It had not been a simple matter for an old man like him who had been so advanced in age and so close to the end of his life even to know about the *Gonghu-in*. It wasn't so surprising, though, that the girl knew about it. She had only listened to an old tale. But for the old man, it was different. I couldn't help but feel anew a sense of respect for him. According to the girl, the old man was from a mountain village in the Province of Hamgyeongdo, and had lived most of his life as a migrant. He had liked to sing old melodies as a pastime.

As she finished, the girl said that she had also grown to like singing the old songs and was certain about wanting to enter a school of Korean classical music, to learn to sing properly. I could tell that she was considerably more mature than she had first impressed me as being. I heard several other things from her: Her family had moved in there because the family business had suddenly failed; her father and mother both worked; she had finished her middle-school education but could not go on to high school, etc. It was too bad that she could not tell us more about the old man, but it was too much to ask of her.

As we were about to leave, I could tell that she wanted to sing something. So I casually asked her to sing something for us that she might have learned from her grandfather. My work would have to wait until the next day, anyway. She had said that she wanted to learn how to sing Korean songs. She readily consented, assumed a professional stance, and added that her grandfather used to hum the song which she was now about to sing, though she had slightly altered it. Her cheeks were flushed the color of silk tree blossoms, and her voice trembled as she sang:

I told him not to cross the river,
But my love crossed nonetheless.
Now that he is drowned and gone,
What will happen next?

As I listened vacantly to it, I was suddenly startled. Was it because I had only been paying attention to the vibrato of her voice? Or was it because I had never heard such a melody before? It hadn't crossed my mind, even as she sang "But my love crossed nonetheless." This couldn't be: The *Gonghu-in* was only known by its lyrics. How was this possible? I stared at her as she finished singing. If the devil didn't have me, someone was making fun of me. But the girl smiled brightly. I was confused. The whole thing seemed phony and fraudulent.

Since the situation had reached a point where the young girl was *singing* the *Gonghu-in*, it was not just phony or fraudulent, it was crazy. My respect for the old man turned into rage. The girl had explained that she had modified the song that the old man used to hum. But this was too much. I felt so humiliated and betrayed, that my face began to twitch. I figured the old man must have been a monomaniac with only a pinch of knowledge about such singing. Even if our weekly did not have "much going for it," we had encountered all kinds of strange and bizarre things. Once there was a middle-aged man who suggested that if anyone followed his method of growing rice, he would harvest twice as much as normal.

I was so pushed out of shape that I turned away from the girl and left without saying a word. In a way, I was grateful to no end that the old man was dead and that we could not interview him. Because we had wasted the day, I would have to stay up all night the next day. So, fortunately, I would avoid getting pressed like a slice of dried squid. Later, I learned from my friend that the entire slum of cardboard shacks had been torn down. But I was so disgusted with the whole business that I paid no mind to it whatever. And then, as I got back to business and the days turned like cogs on a gear, I forgot everything, down to the last trace.

♥

It was one of those nights. After work, I was doing some so-called "light drinking" with my co-workers. I was unusually tired that day, so I slipped away from the gathering. Normally, I also never did such a thing. I walked toward the Sejong Performing Arts Center, where I could catch a bus home. It was still fairly early in the evening, and the moon had cast a faint light in the sky above the streetlights. In those days, the political situation was chaotic, and our company was being catapulted into an unpromising situation. I was thinking about the uncertainty of my future, and there was nothing promising that I could think of. Heck, aren't we supposed to get three chances in life? Well, where was my first? What the hell was going on? It seemed so hopeless. I had been pacing back and forth at the bus stop for a long time, but I hadn't seen one. What time was it, anyway? I walked toward the electronic clock at the front of the building, to check the time. That's when it happened. I spotted the *flying beings*, sculpted in relief on the wall of the Sejong Center. I couldn't tell whose work it was, but it was an adaptation of what was on the temple bell. When the Sejong Center was completed, I seemed to recall clearly from a report about it, the relief on the wall of the building contained representations of the *flying beings*. I halted. I could swear I was watching a *heavenly lady* come flying down off the sculpture. She seemed very far away and yet very close. This *heavenly lady* was alive. I could almost hear the sound of the *gonghu* she was holding and plucking, as her clothing fluttered in the wind. And with it, the sounds of *flutes* and *pan pipes*. I stood there quietly for a while.

Then I heard the singing of the *heavenly lady* from up in the sky. It was not a human voice. On the other hand, it might have been: I couldn't say for sure. Her voice modulated delicately and it occurred to me that I had heard it before. As the sound of the *gonghu* grew louder, so did the singing. What sort of a song was it? I listened. It was the dirge, the *Gonghu-in*. The Korean translation of it, originally written with Chinese characters, enveloped me: *Although I told him not to cross the river, my lord crossed it. Now that he is drowned and gone, what will happen next?*

It took just a moment. The song ended, and with it the sound of the *gonghu*. The hands of the *heavenly lady* that had plucked the *gonghu* were hidden in the moonlight. Even so, I could hear her singing. The singing was clearly that of the young girl. Since she had been the only one in the world to let me hear the song, it was only fitting that it would be she. I started to move my lips to sound out what I was hearing. But there was no way I could give voice to this song, which I could hear so vividly in my ears. It was frustrating. The melody, which I could almost grasp, would not come out of my mouth. I felt like a mute. I could only open my mouth a few times, like a goldfish. But it was such an easy and clear song.

So, why was I unable to sing it? However hard I tried to move my lips, it was no use. Then I understood. A song that rings so clearly in the ears is not a real song, but a song of the heart. Even if I remembered it as that of the young girl, it was not just her song at all. It was the song of the ancients, which simply borrowed the soul of the young girl's song: the *Gonghu-in*, sang by Yeo-ok, the wife of Gwagnijago; the *Gonghu-in* of the *heavenly being*, that dwells, deep and remote, in the echo of the temple bell; and the gut-wrenching songs of farewell, that belong to all the people from of old. If this is true, at some point in my life I must have been singing the *Gonghu-in*, even more deeply and remotely than any other rendition had been sung, and playing the *gonghu* in my heart.

Even though this had happened to me, my contact with the Western Region never went beyond knowing that the *gonghu* had originated there. But I began to look at the Western Region in a different light from then on.

♥

I waited for my girlfriend at the "Injured Knee," and as soon as she came in, we got out of there. She looked totally haggard, unlike how she had looked in the morning. She must have fasted all day. And maybe her shoes were uncomfortable, because she walked with noticeable difficulty. When I asked her with some concern if she was not feeling too well, she answered, "Somewhat," and then, after a while, said, "I'm OK." She smiled at me hurriedly and I glimpsed a wilting flower.

"Aren't you hungry?"

"I don't even notice it anymore."

We waited at the crosswalk the way we used to, long ago, and walked across when the signal changed.

"Did you come from home?" she asked.

"Yeah."

It was gradually getting dark. The streets were astir with people anticipating the two days of a long, golden weekend. As we walked along, I was acutely aware of her shuffling. I had no real sense of the "golden" weekend, because I was living with a woman who had had to go into the hospital, taking advantage of the long weekend.

"There wasn't anything else, was there?"

I had a hard time believing that my girlfriend, who had once had a tumor in her uterus, would be able to keep up her good health. I was becoming afraid that she would grow ill, little by little, and wouldn't be able to work for her company.

"What do you mean, anything else?" My girlfriend turned to look at me, her face like a wilting morning-glory.

"I just wanted to know if anything else happened … at the hospital," I mumbled, averting my face.

"No, nothing else." Because of her hunger and fatigue, she seemed to drag herself along, but she had not lost her spunk. She added that there were plenty of women in her same condition.

"They told me to bring my guardian." She said this as if it had been a strange thing to be asked. So I asked her what she had done about it.

"I told them you were out of town, on business. It's only a formality, you know."

The daylight, like fog, was being pushed out by the darkness. We turned a corner.

"And then, nothing else happened. I just lay there." Her words seeped into the darkness, like fog.

"That was lucky. Never again…." My own words were being lost as they chased after hers, which were disappearing like fog. I shut my mouth. After a hard day's work, she was still filled with a joy that could light up like a little light bulb. I felt sorry for her. I stopped in front of a restaurant, feeling miserable.

"Is this place okay?"

She must have been aware of the place already. Her line of sight was directed toward the entrance, and then she turned to me gently.

"Nothing has changed, has it?"

"No."

When I had suggested that we dine out on the way back from the hospital, she had been as fresh as freshly watered flowers in a garden. Even the expense for our dinner would have to be borne by her, who had to hurry off to work every morning, just as she bore paying the allowances she gave me. Even so, she was happy.

We had frequented this restaurant a number of times before we started living together, as she enjoyed eating meat quite a bit. The sign and the decoration at the entrance were still the same as before.

"Would you prefer the upstairs?" The young man who had been standing in the entrance pointed to the stairs. A young woman led us up. We followed her quietly, as though on our way to listen to a long story.

"Here we are."

It was a cozy room with a small table. As we settled onto our chairs, the young woman brought glasses and some small, damp towels, and set them on the table. My girlfriend opened up a towel and wiped her hands.

"What would you like?" The young waitress asked.

"What should we have?" I looked at my girlfriend and then ordered some meat and a bottle of *soju*. Since we were already in the restaurant, there was no need for me to ask her what she would like to order. As the waitress turned and was on her way out of the room, I added, "A bottle of cola, too." My girlfriend leaned back against the chair, looking drowsy from her fatigue and hunger, which seemed to be overcoming her. It was the first time we had met downtown since the newspaper company I had worked for folded.

I recalled our time together before our cohabitation. Our relationship had been opposed by both families. My relationship with her had always felt unrealistic to me, even up until the last minute before we decided to live together. I had just hung around, never making any decision. I must have tried to run away from her even at that last minute. But something like destiny—to use an elegant expression—prevented me from doing so. Just before we started our life together, I disappeared for a week, for the last time. But I couldn't help but go back to her.

♥

I had suggested that we go out for some fresh air, and I had watched to see if she had changed in any way. But she had been completely devoid of expression. Sitting back against the sightseeing boat, she had only wanted to know where Bong-eunsa Temple might be. I looked toward a wooded area across the river. I figured it must be over there, but I didn't have confidence enough to point it out with any certainty. The rows of high-rise apartment buildings along the river were cut by the Yeongdong Bridge, and there was a dense forest. I was thinking of the lotus blossoms and the Four Deva Kings of Bong-eunsa Temple, and I thought our past meetings had been like some inexplicable pilgrimage.

"It must be somewhere behind those woods." My response was halfhearted. She seemed to accept it. She never mentioned a word about my disappearance the week before. She had never been so indifferent about my whereabouts before. I guessed she must have been a little turned off. But it would have indeed been strange if she really hadn't cared at all to know anything about it. Anyway, she didn't make a peep, for some reason. When I had called her at work, she had asked me if I had been sick. The people where I worked were all upset. I told them that I had not been sick, but I didn't want to divulge what I had done. No one would believe that I had been to a Buddhist temple by myself, missing work at the newspaper for a week. Such capriciousness on my part did not even make sense to me. Yeah, I just had something to take care of. I just had to fudge it.

"When I was a student, I used to walk on the sand a lot, to get to Bong-eunsa Temple after we crossed the river by boat." She looked around, mumbling as if talking to herself. It was apparent that she did not trust her own memory of her trips to the temple during her school days, because the changes that had taken place made the whole area just too unfamiliar.

Though unrelated to how she was feeling, the thought passed through my mind that if she had come here as a student, she must have been in the company of a male student. Then I suspected that when she had been going around the temples with me—to Bongguksa in Jeongneung or Chilbosa in Samcheongdong—she might actually have been reminiscing about those other old days. Sorimsa Temple in Segeomjeong was where we often went. It wasn't that there was anything special about the temple. We hadn't attended any Buddhist lectures or even bowed or prayed to Buddha. When it came to religion, the subject of our discussions while on our way to and from the temple had more to do with Jesus.

The main reason I brought up Jesus was because she had been a seminary student; but she would only listen, whatever it was that I talked about. I talked over a range of subjects, beginning with *La vie de Jésus* by Ernest Renan and the theology of Bultmann and on to the non-denominational movement of Uchimura Kanzou and Ham Seokheon. Of course, I did not have any fixed ideas about Jesus or the church in mind. Even if we were just out for a walk to kill time, I only meant to shorten the trip for her on our way to the Buddhist temple. As I have said, it was something of a mysterious pilgrimage.

Before she and I really knew each other, I visited the room she rented in Segeomjeong all the time. On the way back from Sorimsa Temple, we would often stop at some run-down drinking place along the road and have a drink, usually *makkeoli* or *soju*. On such evenings, I was reminded of the times I used to roam there alone, looking for a room to rent. That's why, when I learned that she was living there alone in a rented room, I saw it as a realization of my dream, vicariously brought about through her. Can I even call it a dream? It was nothing more simple than a desire to leave home and live by myself. But in those days, I was desperate to pull this off, even before worrying about my future or how I would make a living. I was just desperate to rent a room. It was a plan of escape that had no realistic possibility of fulfillment. I have no idea even now why I chose the Segeomjeong area.

It was late autumn, 1964, when I went over the hill through Jahamoon Gate and took a look at Segeomjeong. I was a senior in high school and I had never been there before. In those days, it was still an area of Seoul that was fairly isolated. A drizzle, like a mist, was coming down, off and on, all day, but it wasn't gloomy. The entire basin of Segeomjeong was sunk in fog, and dream-like. If I might use an expression I learned much later, it resembled an oriental wash drawing, meant to impart a dream-like quality to a landscape: to the mountains, water, clouds, and fog. Whenever I imagined myself leaving home and situating myself there somewhere, I was overcome by a secret excitement, and I would tremble.

As the bus climbed up the hill with Jahamoon Gate on the right, a storm of yellow-green leaves tinged with red, perhaps from a zelkova tree, were being blown about by the wind. A village, almost unreal, appeared before my eyes. I can't deny that the reason Segeomjeong has such special meaning to me has a lot to do with how I felt at the time. In spite of the air that the village had of being so deep, so sunken, the hills surrounding it struck me as being a series of crevices, hewn with an ax. Even now, if one goes down into the basin and looks up at the outline of Mt. In-wangsan, one can get a glimpse of Gyeomjae's technique of chiaroscuro, used in his painting, *In-wangjesaekdo*, which shows a "storm lifting, over Mt. In-wangsan."

The bus sped down the hill on the relatively narrow road and stopped at the creek. Leaves were scattering, swept by the wind, and water dripped from the trees. It left me with grave forebodings. I got off the bus and stood under a tree. Unconsciously, I put my hand up to the bill of my school cap. Was I trying to calm myself down? I was a senior in high school and within the month about to go on my last school vacation. But I was still wearing my uniform and school cap. Did I truly come here to look for a place to live, and was it possible to do so? I looked around. The houses had been washed down by the rain and looked much cleaner than when I had seen them from up on Jahamoon Hill. Their brightness made my chest tighten, as I had absolutely no idea as to what I would do.

To make a long story short, nothing happened. Which was to be expected. Whatever the reason, the disappointment one endures after not being able to leave home in spite of such a desperate attempt as an adolescent is truly great. I managed to realize this dream much later, in a different way, but by then I was able to support myself. I attempted to leave home several times. It was like a chronic condition that broke out from time to time, a real nuisance.

Once, I almost followed after a young fellow whom I met in a drinking joint and who informed me that he kept honey bees. He was drunk. Slurring his words, he told me that the earliest flowers to bloom in the spring in Korea are rape, on the island of Jejudo. As spring moves northward, the acacia blooms in April, followed by the chestnut in May. But bush clover blooms first in Kang-won-do Province, at the end of July. He told me that he was spending his life following these flowers. Somehow, what he said was so poignant that I clung to him and begged him to take me along. But he never showed up when we had agreed to meet. I had been so determined that I had packed a backpack, but in the end I clomped home after a sleepless night on a nearby hillside. And then there was that failed attempt to leave for the islands of *Gyeognyeol-bi-yeol-do*. Because of a storm at sea, I could not catch the ferry and had to return home after wandering around the harbor for two solid days.

> *Gyeog-nyeol-bi-yeol-do* (noun) (geo.): An archipelago situated west of Seosan County in Southern Chungcheong-do Province. It tails into Seok-do Island in the east and is at the extreme end of the province. Main industry, fishing. Lighthouse.

This was all I knew about the islands. During the two days of the storm, I met a woman, but only on the second day. When I asked her if she were running away from home without any thought as to where she would go, she answered, casually enough, "Oh, well, I wouldn't call it running away. You rnight say I was just going away on an overnight." From off in the distance, I could hear a mélange of clamoring: the shouting of the stevedores, the long drawn-out drone of a foghorn that abruptly ceases, and the sounds of an anchor being weighed. It didn't register with me as real at all, for everything seemed to swirl around in another place, in a dark world. A road opened the way to the vast ocean between immensely large warehouses. And there was an old sailboat made fast with a manila rope among the motorboats. The sail hadn't been lowered yet, so the patched sail would fill and slacken in the wind. There was nothing more ragged and patched-up than that sail, unless it was my own mind.

She had a longer tongue than I thought. The tongue of a woodpecker. I recalled that a woodpecker pokes its beak into a nest of insects and laps up its prey with its long, sticky tongue. She had the long, thin tongue of a woodpecker. In the morning, I woke up to the long, distant blast of a ship's whistle. My head felt empty. I turned to where she should have been. She was gone. But where could she have gone? I thought she might have gotten up early and gone out for some fresh air. I groped for a cigarette next to the bed and then lit it. I stared blankly at the ceiling. The cigarette smoke scattered as it rose toward the ceiling. I could see that there was a draft. That's why the cigarette smoke was playing in the air. Suddenly, I jumped up and started to pace anxiously back and forth in that narrow room, like some prisoner. I was imprisoned, and the place was empty. I could not figure out who had locked me up and left me there. I shuddered because of a chill in the room, hurriedly put on my jacket, and ran out of the inn as though escaping from it.

The next time I visited Segeomjeong came almost ten years after I finished high school. I had gone up on Jahamoon Hill several times, to pick fruit in the plum orchard and in the pear orchard, and to visit the park, but each of those trips lasted a mere half-day.

When I walked with her to Sorimsa Temple, it wasn't just about Jesus that we talked. My knowledge of Jesus was not very deep, and I sensed that what she was interested in was art rather than Jesus. I had to mobilize everything I knew about it to talk to her. If I didn't open my mouth, there would be a long silence, and so I had to say something. Once, I even had to mention certain literary works such as *Zorba the Greek* by Nikos Kazantzakis and *Demian* by Hermann Hesse. We had also learned about Zen Buddhism, if only superficially, from a scholarly monk at Sorimsa Temple. When she asked him, "Is Zen prayer?," the monk was solemn: "It is different from prayer. One has to struggle through a conundrum in order to arrive at a state where there is a complete absence of desire and thought." His explanation was simple and concise, but he left me at sea.

I was actually more interested in the martial arts of the Chinese. It was obvious that Shaolin Temple in China and Sorimsa Temple in Segeomjeong had no connection, but there were all kinds of films about the martial arts that had the word Shaolin in their titles and this piqued my interest. Such titles ranged from a simple "Shaolin Temple," to "My Cell at Shaolin Temple," "The Wooden Man's Cell at Shaolin Temple," and "The Eighteen Bronze Men of Shaolin Temple"; and even to "The Master Chef of Shaolin Temple," etc. I would be lying if I were to say that all these titles had no influence on me when I thought of Sorimsa Temple in Segeomjeong, even if there was no connection. I can't really pinpoint what it was that accounted for my interest. I am not an expert on the martial arts, and I rarely went out to the movies. So I had no idea what special characteristics or systems the Shaolin school of martial arts had. I assumed that Shaolin was something like what I had watched on TV in the American drama, *Kung Fu*, in which a young man named Kane, who was trained in the Shaolin style of *Kung Fu*, goes around practicing his art in fights against evildoers.

According to the monk at Sorimsa Temple in Segeomjeong, Shaolin in China was the place where Dharma practiced Zen for nine years by facing a wall. This took place at a temple of the Linji Branch, one of the five Zen schools, which is located in Songshan, Dengfeng County, Henan Province. The temple has stone monuments from the Tang and Sung Dynasties, as well as statues of the Three Buddhas of Eastern Wei, and a small chapel named Cuzuan (the Chapel of the First Ancestor) from the Yuan Dynasty. Anyhow, Shaolin Temple in China enjoyed the distinction of being the first Zen temple to be built by Dharma.

When the monk paused for a moment during his explanation, I took the opportunity to ask him how the martial arts had originated at the temple. He looked a little embarrassed.

"I am not suggesting that there is a connection between this temple and that of the Shaolin in China but … wasn't Korean Buddhism influenced by the Chinese?" I went on, to put him at ease. At the same time, names like Maranantha, Soondo (Shundao), and Ado (Yadao) came to mind. He responded, "Well, that's true," but he didn't seem too confident, and hesitated; and then suggested that perhaps the art of disciplining the body to promote physical strength might have developed later into the martial arts. What he meant by later development, he ventured, was that, probably after the Ming Dynasty had failed and the Qing Dynasty was established, a number of patriotic Chinese who considered the Manchurians barbarians congregated at Shaolin clandestinely, to train in the martial arts in the hope of restoring the Ming Dynasty. Although he did provide us with some explanation, he seemed to think I was hopeless, because I was overly concerned with such questions. It was obvious that he was trying to teach me something about Zen every time our eyes met. He was intent on informing us that Dharma had five successors: Hyega (Hui-ke), Seungchan (Sengcang), Doshin (Daoxing), Hong-in (Hongren), and Hye-neung (Huineng); and that there were five lineages of Zen: the Wi-angjong (Weiyangzong), Jodongjong (Caodongzong), Imjejong (Linjizong) , Woonmoonjong (Yunmengzong), and Beop-anjong (Fayangzong).

♥

The sightseeing boat dropped anchor at a place where the bridge piles and the guardrails looked squared above. Because it was the rainy season, there were few boats in the water. From the time the boat anchored, I was annoyed by the loud laughter from a boat on the far side. It was the laughter of middle-aged women exchanging dirty jokes. The owner of the boat, who had rowed out and handled the anchor, had already taken off in a dinghy that had been attached to the side of the boat. He went over to a houseboat where he talked with his wife. Judging by the fact that she went off with a saucepan in hand, she must have been off to order the *maewoontang* that we had ordered. It was supposed to be a combination spicy stew. My girlfriend would probably have preferred a combination of minnows, cornet fish, and carp to the one made simply with catfish or mandarin fish. And I had ordered a bottle of *soju* for myself and a bottle of beer for her. She let me do the ordering and seemed not to care what I ordered.

I couldn't figure out why she seemed like a different person. Was it due to the fact that I had disappeared without a word and come back? When the owner of the boat dropped anchor, I had exclaimed, "He's throwing in the anchor! The anchor!" But she would not show any interest. Then I felt silly that I was attaching so much meaning to an anchor, like some child. An anchor finds its anchorage in the invisible depths of the water. I must have thought that I was in need of such an anchorage. There was no denying that I was yearning for a union in which she would be my anchorage.

"Is the sun too strong?"

The direct sun was blinding. I got up and pulled down one of the blinds that could actually be drawn on every side. I wanted at least to shade our faces.

"That boat over there has all the blinds drawn."

Indeed, one of the three or four boats that were scattered in the distance had their green vinyl blinds drawn, concealing the interior.

"Well, that's just...," I said, rather embarrassed. I thought I had glimpsed a man and a woman on the boat before the blinds were dropped. Were they naked now? The middle-aged women in the nearby boat had started drinking, still boisterous and mirthful. Beyond their cackling, an apartment building in the distant district of Yeongdong appeared to float like a mirage past the Seongsu Bridge. Cars were backed up on the Yeongdong Bridge, and faces looked down on the river from unmoving buses.

♥

When I was young, my little brother and I used to go down to the stream to swim and to skim rocks over the water. One, two, three, four— the stones would swiftly skim over the surface of the water and filled us with delight.

One day, after a swim, we were about to throw some stones while drying off in the sun when a woman came down the slope on the other side. She had long hair and seemed melancholy. Her gaze was lowered, and she was describing circles in the air with a stalk of sorghum. We held off throwing any stones and hid our clothes among the boulders. She was not a young woman, only a girl. When she reached the stream, without a moment's hesitation, she lifted her skirt and squatted. From what we saw, we knew she wasn't wearing anything underneath. My brother and I held our breath and just watched. "Who is she?" my brother whispered in my ear. "Quiet! How the hell should I know, stupid?" I covered his mouth and glared at him, but I knew she lived in the house of one of my classmates. Quite a few young women like her swarmed in and out of his house. At last, the girl used the sorghum to scratch between her legs, appearing to be in some pain. She must have picked up some horrible disease. The bright sunlight shone white between her thighs.

My brother spit and said, "Ugh, she's scratching her scabs. She must have gotten ringworm."

"Shut up, you numbskull. That's not what it is. You only get ringworm on your head." In spite of my trying to keep him quiet, he got up in a flash and shot a stone across the water. Surprised, she got up and hastily pulled her skirt down, staring at us resentfully. We grabbed our clothes and, still naked, went off into the sorghum field to hide. My brother kept spitting.

♥

If my little brother had been there, he would have thrown rocks at the boat with the blinds down. How were they entwined on that boat? Were they entwined like dogs? Or like frogs? Or like snails? Or, rather, were they the color of the earth? Or were they the color of a rose? And, over them, the cackling of the women.

The week before, I suddenly had the urge to leave Seoul, and it might have been a recurring symptom of my old infirmity. After I went to Bongeunsa Temple, I made up my mind to do it. It wasn't necessarily that I was inspired while at the temple. I just happened to see a pond with large lotus leaves on it and the Four Deva Kings standing there with their fierce, glaring eyes. I had no real plans. I just felt the tug of a strong desire to leave Seoul and to find a new life. It was much like the desire I had when I was a senior in high school.

My girlfriend had said to me around that time that she was going to leave Segeomjeong and move near Ddukseom, which was closer to her work. If I had been thinking about leaving her at the time, it must have been a real coincidence. Was I interested in her only because she was renting a room where I wanted to rent and live? And this for several years? Was I trying to relieve my frustration at not being able to realize this simple dream through her? So when she told me that she was going to leave Segeomjeong, did I decide to leave her so that some other frustration of mine might be compensated for by her? That must not have been the case. I simply wanted to get away from myself. That was the only reason.

In fact, I had been so bored that I could not bear it any more. My work was nothing special to me, and my future was much too unclear. At first, I had wanted to see the land that had been set aside for the feeding of cats. I had heard, somewhere, that during the Joseon Period a king had bestowed a number of plots of land which would yield a harvest sufficient to support the raising of cats. Bong-eunsa Temple was said to have been one of the temples that had such specially designated land.

Once, King Sejo of the Joseon Dynasty went to Mount Odaesan in Kang-won-do Province. As he was about to enter the Main Hall of Sang-wonsa Temple, a cat suddenly sprang out before him. The King became suspicious and had the Main Hall of the temple searched. Sure enough, an assassin was hiding in the hall. The King considered that the cat had saved his life and bestowed a plot of land specifically for the upkeep of the cat.

It was unreasonable to look for the plot for cats in a place where small shops lined the way to the very entrance of the temple. I was reminded of another story about a cat that the scholarly monk had told us at Sorimsa in Segeomjeong. I pondered over the story while gazing at the lotus blossoms in the pond.

Once, in China, a Zen monk, Nanquan, killed a cat that his disciples were arguing over. Nanquan later told the story to his disciple, Zhao Zhou, who had been away. After listening to the story, Zhao Zhou quietly took off his shoes, put them on his head, and walked out. "What could this mean?" the scholarly monk asked us. Then he went on: "Well, Master Nanquan killed the cat in order to teach the monks detachment, and Zhao Zhou wanted to show that one should not argue right or wrong using the values of the secular world."

But this doesn't mean that I had reached the point where I was going to sever my attachments and ties to the secular world. I felt no conviction that I should lead a new life, but simply a disillusionment about the tedious and monotonous life I did have. Was it her fault? No, it wasn't. Not too long before, to be with her was my greatest joy. Nevertheless, I had to leave her. I couldn't even say, well, because I love her, I have to leave her, as one so often finds in popular songs. I just needed to leave. How can I explain such unfathomable and immoral behavior?

♥

The owner of the boat rowed over in his dinghy and set down the tray with the *maewoontang* soup, *soju*, and beer on it, and took off again. I opened the bottles with an opener that was attached to the side of the boat. She just watched me. A few fish floated in the pot like upturned boats on the beach. I asked myself, "Am I suffering?" The answer was, no.

"Shall we play a word game? You know, tell funny stories?" I suggested, lifting my glass. Her eyes twinkled. I figured she had no idea that I was going to say goodbye. I was a little sad, but relieved. I was going to propose our separation, but I wasn't about to conclude our relationship with an opening like, "Why don't we break up?" I was hoping we would *communicate without words* and *understand each other intuitively*, the way the Zen Buddhists speak of doing. What a laughable idea!

"Do you know the reason why Jesus came into this world and bore the cross?"

"Jesus?"

"Yeah." I felt miserable, and regretted having suggested the game. But it was too late. She turned to me, with a faint smile on her face.

"A big-cone pine tree in the front yard." Her voice rang clearer than ever. I was at a loss for words. A big-cone pine tree in the front yard! That was the same kind of answer that the Zen master, Zhao Zhou, gave to the question, "Why did Dharma come from the west?" Asking "Why did Dharma come from the west?" was like asking, "What are the fundamental principles of Buddhism?" and "What is the Tao, the Way to Enlightenment?" When I asked her my question, I was expecting her answer to be something like what Jesus had said: "Do not put the Lord your God to the test."

"That's way too hard for a game," I protested, as gently as possible and with a smile. But she did not smile.

"If you ask me a hundred questions at a time, I will give you straight answers."

"So, that's it!"

I had totally botched it. What she had said was also taken from a Zen master's talk. At this point, our word game—communicating without words; that is, intuitively understanding each other—was totally useless. We had never discussed Zen, even on our trip to Sorimsa Temple in Segeomjeong. And I had no idea when she had read the teachings of the Zen masters, either. Then I realized that I would never be able to suggest that we separate if the word game continued. I recalled the times that we had gone to Sorimsa Temple. I had always thought about leaving her. But I could not understand it. I had always plotted to depart from everything but was never able to. And even from her, I was not able to. It was possible that our meeting and separating were tightly bound by the two opposing forces: the centrifugal and the centripetal. At least for a while, I would not consciously contrive to leave her.

Sorimsa Temple came to mind. Then I asked myself, "Where is Sorimsa Temple?"

Where was Sorimsa Temple? Was it in China, on Mount Xiungshan? I couldn't think of an answer. Sorimsa Temple was neither in Segeomjeong nor in Song Shan.

Then where was it?

It was in my mind. I just didn't know where my mind was. I was totally spent, and I didn't dare think of continuing the word game with her. I just poked around in the saucepan. I fished out a goby minnow, stuffed its head in my mouth, and began chewing it up. Not long after that, we started living together, rather casually.

Under these circumstances, even the newspaper I worked for folded, and there was nothing I could do about it. Before I could blame society, I myself had become so helpless, everything was hopeless. We were lucky we still had our lease on the room. It was in a neighborhood that was always astir with a din or clamor: the sound of alarms going off, of running water, of loud arguments, of dogs barking, of nagging women shrieking, of Christian singing, and of loud speakers. Against all this noise, the back room that we had was reasonably quiet, as if it were slightly detached from everything. Because the house was located in a neighborhood on a hillside, we could look out the window and catch a glimpse of the evening sunset, and at times see people on bicycles coasting downhill on the other side. But it had lots of other shortcomings. When we were looking for a place to rent, the real estate agents showed us places farther up the hill, and tears formed in her eyes when we got pretty high up. The room had a stove underneath the floor, but the heat did not warm the room very well. When the cold weather came, we put in an iron bed and a stove that burned coal-blocks. It was pretty pathetic.

♥

A griddle was heating up on the portable gas-burner. The bottles of *soju* and cola had been opened. While my girlfriend silently put the thin slices of meat on the griddle, I silently poured some liquor into a glass. It seemed like a ritual.

"While I was in the recovery room, three other people came in."

I poured some cola in her glass.

"It was horrible."

My girlfriend pressed the meat as it cooked, with her chopsticks. I could hear the fan going. The bubbles on the inside of her glass of cola, looking like transparent insect eggs, started burbling up.

"I didn't even get to see the doctor. I was waiting to see if the doctor would show up, but they said that it was all over."

She turned over several pieces of meat. As she drank her cola, I kept pace, drinking my *soju*.

"Let's go to Seokguram Grotto next time we have a long weekend."

I don't know why, out of the blue, I said Seokguram. I surprised myself. But there was no answer from her. I was wondering if she were thinking Seokguram was some kind of restaurant, rather than the

Seokguram in Gyeongju.

"Maybe my anesthesia was too strong. The woman next to me told me that she could even hear the scraping."

She picked up a piece of meat with her chopsticks. She said she was so hungry, her stomach actually hurt.

"You go ahead and eat. I'll just drink for a while."

"Have some appetizers with your drink."

"I will, later." I poured my glass to the brim. She was busy chewing.

"Meat has to be eaten with salad to be well digested."

♥

Just before I finished middle school, our class went on a school trip to Tohamsan in Gyeongju, in order to see the Seokguram Grotto at sunrise. We weren't able to see it, as the sky had clouded over. We were very disappointed, since we had had to get up early and huff-andpuff our way up the mountain. Obviously, we weren't able to see the face of the stone Buddha very well. Neither the stone robes on the eleven Guanyin Boddhisatvas in bas-relief, which are said to resemble angels' garments, nor the arch over the grotto, which appears to be woven in stone like a piece of cloth, registered in our consciousness.

♥

The reason I had suddenly blurted out Seokguram must have been because of my association of it with the Dunhuang Caves.

"I don't know if I should drink so much cold cola. Would it be all right to have another one?"

"I'm sure it's okay."

She rang the bell, which was on the wall next to the door to the room. A waitress appeared almost simultaneously, and my girlfriend ordered another bottle of cola.

"What did you do during the day?"

"I slept." I poured the garlic cloves onto the hot griddle.

"All that time?"

"Yeah. I sure got the most out of that iron bed."

"They say that sleeping too much is not good for you. The more you sleep, the sleepier you get."

"Shall I lower the heat? They're burning."

I bent over to check the fire and slowly reduced it. I could sense the alcohol spreading through my body. The smoke was being sucked up into the ventilator on the ceiling. We ate and drank for a while without speaking.

"Would you like anything else?" the waitress asked when she brought in the cola.

"We still have quite a bit. Maybe later," I answered.

My girlfriend must have been thirsty, for she emptied her glass in one gulp. After the waitress left, we ate and drank for a while withou speaking a word. Obviously, the dinner was meant for her benefit.

"I had a dream while I was asleep." I filled my glass again. I started to make up a story.

"Oh, well. Having a dream while you nap is not something to ..."

My girlfriend gave her dreams considerable credence. If you dream of a pig, it has to do with money. If you dream of someone dead, it is a sign of good fortune. If you dream of the moon, it indicates a pregnancy.

"I often have dreams on *that ol' iron bed*."

She laughed at my expression, *that ol' iron bed*. She was wrapping some rice in a lettuce leaf, but stopped.

"How come? What's wrong with the iron bed? Are you having nightmares?"

I had not had any dreams for a long time. I used to think that if you start losing your hopes and dreams in reality, you will also stop dreaming when you sleep. She offered me the little ball of rice wrapped in the lettuce leaf.

"Try this. Lettuce helps you sleep well."

"No, I ..."

"Come on, you won't have any more nightmares."

She held the wrapped rice ball out to me. I opened my mouth like a child and took it. Then she asked, "Isn't it good?" I scowled, deliberately.

"What did you dream about?"

"On that ol' iron bed...," I started to say, but I could not finish until I had swallowed the rice in the lettuce leaf.

"I had such strange dreams."

"Oh, really? What did you dream about?"

She blinked, as if she were imagining to herself dreams of money, health, and good luck.

"Today, I dreamed about dancing." I grinned. As I expected, she was interested.

"Did you say, 'dancing'?"

"That's right."

She was so amused, she giggled. "You don't know how to dance. You can't even dance disco, can you? And you were dancing?"

"If I knew how to dance, why would I dream about it? I dance in my dreams because I don't know how."

"That's a nightmare."

Her mouth moved constantly as she chewed her meat, but she did not stop smiling. I was desperately hoping that she would not stop smiling, at least for the day, until she went home and fell peacefully asleep.

"Was it disco?" There was something innocent about her curiosity.

"No."

"What then?"

"Something like it."

"What might that be?"

"It was a lion dance. A lion dancing, with a flying mane. So it wasn't I who was dancing. It was a lion, and I was just watching."

I quickly regretted it, thinking I should have come up with a different dance. But I couldn't have thought up anything else, even if I'd had the time.

"The lion was attacking me—as it danced."

"I wonder what a lion in a dream means. Anyhow, it was a good dream," my girlfriend decided.

"The lion would not stop. It kept on dancing and shaking its head. I went up to it and grabbed its bridle, but it wouldn't stop. Was it still a good dream?" I pretended to snatch the bridle.

"I would think so. But did you say, bridle? Did the lion have on a bridle?"

"Is that bad?"

"I don't know. I don't think so."

Pushing some scorched meat off to a corner of the griddle, she seemed to let herself sink into the significance of the lion's dance.

"I tried hard to grab the bridle, but I just didn't have the strength. I tried as hard as I could, but my hands froze shut." I closed and opened my hand.

"What happened after that?"

"I woke up worrying about how to stop the lion."

She had probably never dreamed of a lion. If she had ever dreamed of one, she would not have kept quiet about it.

"That's a *dog* dream and it doesn't mean anything." She laughed helplessly.

"I told you I dreamed about a *lion*."

"It's what a *dog* would dream about."

She put the rest of the meat on the plate onto the griddle and turned up the gas. I picked out a clove of garlic that was burnt like a chunk of black rubber.

"I think the lion might still be dancing, even now."

"Let it dance if it wants."

The room was filled with the smell of the meat cooking and with the heat from the griddle.

"I don't dream these days. Once, for us to have different dreams while we slept in the same bed would have made me feel strange and remote."

I stared at her. Her face had a dreamlike quality, flushed in the vapor of the oil that was rising as though in some mirage.

"You know, the three of us would have had to sleep on that narrow bed this winter." She laughed loudly, sounding like a dabchick.

"What are you talking about? How could three of us sleep on it? And besides, there are still just two of us."

The summer sun, beating wildly on the slate roof, was already descending, and autumn was in the air. I hoped that my girlfriend would not lose her smile and that her heart would not grow cold. She no longer looked at the griddle.

"Why don't you have some more? Don't you want to?" I said, to coax her.

"It's good, but I can't eat the way I used to. And I just ate. If you don't want this, how about some rice?"

"No. I don't eat rice when I drink. If you want some, go ahead and order it."

"No, no, I'm fine." She shook her head and took a sip of the *mulkimchi* juice. I was ready to drink some more, but the bottle had been empty for a while.

"Let's go to Seokguram sometime." Finally, I said it again.

"Why, suddenly, to Seokguram?" Life returned to her eyes again.

"Why? To go sightseeing in Gyeong-ju. You've never been to Gyeong-ju, have you?"

"No. I've never been there."

"I was there once. But I was so young that I didn't know what was what. Why don't we go there, next time we get a long weekend."

The door opened and the waitress came in. "Shall I turn off the burner?" Before we could answer, she had turned off the gas and put out the flame. Anyhow, for a while my girlfriend had just been picking up her wooden chopsticks and setting them down again.

"Would you give me a plastic bag so we can take this home?" my girlfriend asked, looking up at the waitress.

"Would you like the check, too?"

My girlfriend turned toward me. I nodded to the waitress and she went out quietly.

"Why don't you finish it?"

My girlfriend shook her head, drank the last bit of cola at the bottom of her glass, and then wiped her mouth. "I've never eaten so much. I shouldn't have gorged myself after fasting like that. It might give me indigestion. I need to go home and rest."

The waitress came with the plastic bag and check, and slid them onto the table. I picked up the check, examined it, and passed it to my girlfriend. She looked at it for a moment and said, with apparent satisfaction, "It's cheap." I had only pretended to look over the check, and had no idea how much the bill was. She picked up the few remaining pieces of meat, one by one, and put them in the plastic bag. I got up from the table and waited a long time in the hallway near the stairs for her to come out.

"Today's been a long day," she said as she was going down the stairs. It was true. But somehow that long day did not seem real to me, and I looked at her once again as though to confirm that it was real.

Even when we were getting out of the taxi at the foot of the hill in our neighborhood, I could not shake this sense of unreality. She had been dozing off in the taxi. When the taxi stopped and her body swayed forward in reaction to it, she asked, "Are we here already?" and looked around: I had hardly any sense that, indeed, it had been a long day.

Clearly, our familiar neighborhood was what was real. She still walked awkwardly the way she had when we had come out of the Injured Knee. I put my hand under her arm to support her. Although she kept telling me, "I'm okay, I'm okay," she seemed to appreciate the help. Under the streetlamps, our shadows were stretched so far out, it seemed they were hesitating to climb the steep slope. I thought of us as returning from a long trip. But from where? Perhaps from somewhere outside of reality? As we passed a lamppost, our shadows went ahead, leading the way.

"Wouldn't life really be tedious if every day were this long?" she asked, leaning against me.

"If love did not exist, it might be true."

"Do you think so?" Her words seemed distant, as if emanating from a shadow. She sounded exhausted.

We turned the key and opened the door. As soon as we were in our room, she threw herself onto the bed without fully undressing.

"Sometimes a day can be very long…. "

I picked up the desk clock, which had stopped, and wound it up. I lifted her wrist to check her watch. It was 11 o'clock. I set the hands on the desk clock and turned toward the bed, but she was already asleep.

All of a sudden, it was still, all around. Could it be an airplane? A hum reverberated in the room, from close by and from off in the distance. The earth might also have been flying in the dark, to the sound of a solitary engine.

I sat on a corner of the bed and lit a cigarette. It had been a long day. It had been a long day for her as well. A sense of fatigue, as if I had made a long journey on foot, overcame me like a wildfire. My heart stirred with a sense of incomprehensible remorse. I had to rest, for I had made such a long journey. A long journey, a long day. Everything was now past. I had to sleep. But I couldn't. I raised my eyes to the road that stretched before me. It stretched far out before me, thirty-thousand *li* to the west of China. Then I thought of the lion's dance. "What? Did I say I dreamed of a lion?" I smirked. Laughter slipped from my lips and I chuckled. I was surprised at how loud my own laughter was. Then I stifled it. I gagged, barely managing to stop it.

She was sound asleep under the bright electric light. It had been a long day. The room was a stage, with a curtain backdrop. I turned off the light. It was dark, but white light poured in through the window. It was moonlight. "How bright the moonlight is…," I murmured.

The moonlight on the corner of the bed reflected and shone on her aching feet. The soles were made white. "I want at least to have my socks on when I have the procedure," she had said in the morning, as she packed a pair of white socks. She was asleep with her feet in the moonlight, and wore only a slip. Was it the moonlight that made her body seem to float in the air on the iron bed, the way it would in a magic show? If I were to take away the bed, she would probably stay right there, suspended by herself in the air. Or, perhaps she was on her way somewhere, her feet bathed in the brimming moonlight. I put out my cigarette, which had burnt down to the filter, by crushing it in the ashtray, and started to pace the floor. The room, ten feet long by nine feet wide, contained these things: a spindly sprig of sweet-pea, wilting in a glass on the bookcase; a plastic wardrobe, supported by fitted steel bars, which resembled a portable changing room; and a few onions in the corner of the cupboard. Centipedes must have been crawling on the window frame. I never did anything to them, but I found them dead, curled up in the track of the sliding window, when I opened it in the mornings.

I was thirsty. I picked up the teakettle off the top of the low cupboard and gulped down some water. Suddenly, the moonlight in the room was gone. The clouds must have hidden the moon. I went up to the window and looked out. A cloud was passing over the moon, which looked like a round tray made of white brass. Did I hear sand scratching the tray? I could not believe my ears.

My wish to go to Seokguram was one of deep yearning. But there was little chance that such an opportunity would come. Even if such an opportunity were to present itself, I was aware that I would not be able to go into the grotto, because they had built an anteroom in front of it. I looked down the hill. It looked like a desert washed white in the moonlight. The curtain had fallen after a long day, and the moon was traveling across the desert. The long journey, thirty-thousand *li*, to the Western Region. The rock caves of the desert were also soaked in the moonlight. I had no reaction when my friend told me about the caves at Dunhuang. Even if it were true that Hyecho had chanted the Hymn of Self-Enlightenment in the Western Region and had written his "Journey to the Western Region" there, I felt no connection to that region. Even if the culture of the Western Region had exerted one of the greatest influences on our arts and culture, I felt it to be something useless nothing more than an exotic flavor. I had felt this as I was leaving home in the afternoon. When I was making up the story about dreaming about a lion, I felt the same way. But I knew what was going on. Even if I hadn't dreamed about a lion on the iron bed, I had long been dreaming about a dancing lion. It was true. The lion wasn't just the Lion in the Bukcheong Mask Dance, which bestowed longevity. The lion was the one in the Sanye of Silla, as well as the one in the murals of the Dunhuang caves.

A Lion, with a face like the sun, sauntered out into the street, nodding up and down to the rhythm of a marching band. Its paws were wide apart and it looked to the left and to the right, and began to dominate the stage, swaggering from place to place. Tum, Tum, Tum, Tum, Tum, Tum. It trembled and shook its mane. It ran about until it was exhausted. Before that, it kept up its round.

Tum, Tum, Tum, Tum, Tum, Tum.

The sky seemed to brighten again, as if it were a reflection in the snow. My girlfriend was still in bed, sound asleep, motionless. She was like a doll made of wax on a stand: Only her pale outline rose up out of the dark. Now moonlight filled the room. Asleep like the dead, she would probably become an eternal mummy, soaked in moonlight. And it would be said that she was "a female mummy, dressed in the very style of the twentieth century, having been discovered buried in moonlight. The archeologists and scientists who study the human body and the nature of light will deem the mummy to have been preserved as perfectly as it was, by the condensed moonlight, which prevented the corruption of the body. This mummy, tagged 'The Girl of Seoul,'is ..."

I stood right next to the bed and looked down at her. "The Girl of Seoul" was walking in the desert on her aching feet. I squatted on the floor and pressed my lips to her foot. Had she moved her toes? No, she hadn't. But when I got up, she suddenly turned over. I was nervous that she might have been aware of what I had done. My heart pounded like a young boy's.

"I'm thirsty," I said loudly, and went over to the cupboard and groped for the teakettle. It was about a third full. "Not a drop of water in it!" She made no response. I opened the door and went out. Just outside our room was the kitchen, under the overhang of the roof. It was a supposed to be a kitchen, but it was really an open space without walls. I stepped onto the cement floor in my barefoot and turned on the faucet to fill the kettle. I pretended to drink from it. Then, I set it down near the drain.

Were you asleep the whole time?

Yeah, I was dreaming. I was dreaming of dancing.

It was a moonlit night. A lion was making its way across a faraway desert, under the moonlight. Weighted down by its own heaviness, it went silently up and over the sand dunes. It walked at a very slow pace. Swish ... swish.... Was this the sound of sand sliding down the slopes of Mount Mingshashan? The lion simply moved its legs, one after the other, without paying attention. Even its tracks were buried by the sand. As the moonlight became brighter, its entire body was covered by the light as though by silver scales held together with glue. There was not a twinkle of light as far as the eye could see. In the midst of the desert, there was only the shadow of the lion, which moved ever so slowly. The world was still, absolutely still. Even the shadow seemed still as it moved. But the lion kept walking without letup. The silver scale of the moon had faded like the metallic finish of an old watch. The distant past revealed itself as a desert, and the lion kept walking in it, never stopping. There was no end to the desert of time. Only the lion kept its pace, its eyes on its paws.

Did it pass through Loulan?

Did it pass through Dunhuang?

The lion is walking silently through the infinite void, which has no end. Each time it moves its paw, we hear the sound of it in the sand. Do I hear the sound of sand shifting under the moonlight? Or is it the sound of sand being swept away by time? Or is it, still, the sound of the *gonghu*, which has traveled, resonating, the thirty- thousand *li* from the Western Region?

Someone mumbled something just then. Hey, kid. If it was a boy, think of him as having gone to a faraway place, seeking the Way, like Hyecho. If it was a girl, think of her becoming pretty in the desert. Think of that alone.

The lion halted. I wondered what was the matter. Suddenly, the lion asked, "Is Bongsan a long way from here? Is Gangnyeong very far away? Is Girin very far away?"

Startled, I simply shook my head. At the same time, the lion raised its eyes, which were huge and glaring.

"Who are you? Aren't you the uncle from Bukcheong?"

The lion flung aside its skin as soon as it finished speaking.

"Indeed, it has been a long day. Isn't this perhaps the first time that you have ever danced so much?"

The voice was hoarse, as though sand had been caught in its throat. But I could guess whose voice it was.

It was my own.

♥

The Love of Loulan

A few years ago when I was just getting interested in the subject of Dunhuang and Loulan, I was living with a woman. My life with her in that room was not going anywhere: The days simply passed. Even in living this way, I was caught up in certain thoughts about Dunhuang, Loulan, and the lion. Loulan was, like Dunhuang, the name of a city-state which had been an oasis in western China but is now a ruin.

Our life together in that damp and lightless room would be better described as cohabitation, even if the meaning might ultimately be the same. We were simply inhabiting the place together rather than sharing a life. The whole time, we were stuck in that dark room. We grew pale and sank into a dark world that was all our own. This does not mean that we were absorbed in carnal pleasures either, as people might easily imagine. We were living, even in such a small room, as if we were passing ships. The carnal pleasures were past, like the heat of a season. Like words regarding sex found in the dictionary, they lay dormant in the folds of my brain.

I kept wanting to do something meaningful, and summer was passing without anything meaningful happening. But we could not get out of that room. My urge to leave wasn't just because of some compulsion about living. At last, I suggested we free ourselves from the room, if only for a day.

Toward the end of August, suddenly, there were a few days with deep blue skies. Was it fall already? The weather was still very hot and muggy.

"I was in Pusan when Typhoon Sarah hit." I made this completely off-the-wall remark as we were heading for the beach.

"Typhoon Sarah?"

"Yeah, the typhoon. It was really terrible."

I was exaggerating, as if begging to be recognized as someone who had experienced a great historical event. In truth, Typhoon Sarah was terrible. Had it happened during the holiday for the Harvest Moon Festival? If not, it must have been very close to it. I found out that the typhoon bore an American girl's name, Sarah, much later. I had watched in my room as roof-tiles flew off and telephone posts fell over. As soon as the wind stopped, I ran out of the house and saw how the landscape had changed completely from the way I had known it for such a long time. When I went out onto the highway, I could see potholes here and there, and plane trees uprooted and strewn about. The windowpanes of all the houses were dazzling and made the houses seem empty. Although the storm had stopped, the stream was overflowing and muddy. People say that nothing is more exciting than watching a fire, a flood, or a fight. I never saw so much water, either before or after that time.

A great many people were watching the raging water on either side of the stream, excitement showing on their faces. Actually, they were fighting the water. Using a hook on the end of a pole, people fished out things that were floating downstream. Doors and doorposts, even roofs floated by on the water. Some people, it was said, even fished out a few pigs. Some saved others who were riding the current holding onto a board. Some grown-ups told us that people who float along on the current are bothered the most by snakes. Apparently, snakes in the water attach themselves to people. I never witnessed anything like that that day, but I used to shudder after having nightmares in which someone, a snake coiled around his body, was drifting downstream, petrified. Snakes bored into every orifice of his body. My watching such a thing meant that I was next. What a horrid thing to dream!

Why was I thinking of a typhoon as I headed for the beach at the end of August? The sky was clear and the sun was shining. But I was secretly expecting stormy weather and a high surf. Actually, this was less secret than it was intense.

It was already past the height of the season for summer vacations. School vacations were over, or at least at the tail end, and companies had also had their vacations. Even the newspapers that had raved, "Crowd the Largest Human Wave Since Opening," and had talked of hundreds of thousands of people had now turned their cameras elsewhere. In a newspaper photo, "Aerial View of Haewoondae Beach, from Helicopter," several hundreds of thousands of people were spread out like so many little dots. All these men and women, who suffer from the desire to be loved, appeared only as dots. This had been only a few days before.

But now the newspapers were finishing up their reporting on summer vacation with an article saying that some people were "making a profit" hunting for coins on the beach. People were combing the sand on the beach with rakes, like the pig in *A Journey to the West*. Then they said that all the lost coins had been raked in. There were more than a few coins, and this treasure hunting was becoming a "new enterprise." Not only coins but also other metal objects such as rings and watches had also been found in some quantity.

When I saw this report, I was suddenly reminded of a time before when I had gone to the beach with a girl. I was just getting out of puberty. If one can say that pure love is the kind of love which is not physically consummated, our love at the time would have been considered pure love. What is Platonic love? I did wonder whether it was something that completely excluded sex. Soon I discovered in my own way that even Platonic love was an immature expression of a yearning for sex, and I also learned of the sad reality that Socrates, the philosopher who was Plato's teacher, fell in love homosexually while suffering because of a bad wife. Until then, I believed love was the skill to hide one's hunger and desperate yearning for sexual love, as if one didn't know about it. How could one perpetrate such a beastly act upon the woman one loves?

We were walking on the beach in that kind of relationship of love. It was also just after the peak season of summer vacation. It was our first time going to the beach. Each of us had already been to the beach on our own. We had gone to the beach each with our own friends, and we had enjoyed talking about it. Whenever we talked about our trips to the beach, I would visualize her having fun, frolicking on the beach wearing a bikini. Even so, for some reason, we never suggested to one another that we ourselves go swimming together. I must have thought it was taboo, since such a proposal might have sounded as if I wanted to see her undressed. Taking off our clothes seemed to me to be an insult to love. After walking on the beach, we sat down on a low sand dune and looked out at the far horizon without saying anything. We must have been gazing out at the deep sea, filled with merriment and thinking of our encounter, of love, and of happiness.

This must have been …

When the word "love" came to mind, I felt myself grow hot in the eyelids. Out of all the myriads of people there are, who are as numerous as grains of sand, how did I happen to meet her? Words such as *fate* and *providence* seemed to make real sense to me. I was becoming short of breath and tight in the chest, and wrapped in true solitude. The blue ocean was a sign that love was moving deep down.

Was I learning what "love" was, at last?

Just then, I saw a number of boys coming our way, searching in the sand. They were poking in the sand with sticks, and at times bent down to pick something up and examine it. You could tell they were not good kids, even at a glance. But it was none of my business. We didn't have anything that would attract them. We were just sitting on the sand bank, looking out at the sea. I glanced at them momentarily and then stared out to sea. We kept silent. As they got nearer, I realized that they were looking for things on the beach. They were looking for articles that vacationers had lost. But they chatted and snickered incessantly, as if finding lost articles wasn't the only thing they were interested in. I felt a little self-conscious and straightened myself uncomfortably, but she kept very still. They passed by in front of us. One of them pretended to search in the sand and muttered out loud so we could hear: "Didn't someone drop a clitoris around here somewhere?"

I was pissed when I heard this. My face frozen, I checked to see how she had taken it, without letting her know; but she appeared completely unaffected, as if she had not even heard it. Perhaps she really had not heard it. Or, possibly, she had not understood the word "clitoris." If that was the case, I was the only one having a hard time stewing over what he had said. I knew all about it because I had read those colored inserts in the popular magazine that you tear open to read. Such things as "The Structure of the Female Sex Organs," as they were called, were elementary, common knowledge. I was an embodiment of evil, having fantasized about the whole ugly world of sexual activity. Sitting next to her, who was so holy and innocent, and who dreamt of true love, I was the dirty male imagining to myself base things like the clitoris.

One newspaper had noted "Autumn Cool on Heels of Summer Heat" and pictured a deserted beach, the crowds of summer gone. Aside from contrasting the summer heat and the autumn coolness, it had pointed out how changeable people are, and how they turn to other things quickly.

She didn't seem to care about the typhoon. Someone who lived in Seoul would never, obviously, care much about typhoons. To the people of Seoul, a typhoon was something that comes and goes only in weather reports, or comes only as a distant news report of how many houses, how much acreage of fields and paddies, or how many lives might have been lost. Furthermore, I was bringing up Typhoon Sarah, something that had happened twenty years ago. No wonder she wasn't interested. Quite a bit of summer was still left and we were headed for the beach. She asked, "Will we be able to swim?," as if asking, "What is a typhoon?" I answered readily: "Of course."

Women divers go into the water even in winter. I had long ago seen such women entering the sea in the winter, clad only in flimsy swimming suits made of cloth, nothing like the kind of sleek wet suits we see these days. Personally, I went swimming for the first time that year in Gwang-al-li in Pusan, when on April 19th, 1960, the April 19th Revolution occurred. I was in middle school and I had gone swimming with a few of my friends. Our lips all turned blue and we had goose bumps all over us, but we still went in and bodysurfed. It was still too early in the season for swimming, but that day it must have been pretty sunny.

Anyhow, I remember April the 19th as the earliest date I ever went swimming in any year. Of course, I didn't know then that anything was happening that day. But that day was the first time I ever saw someone who drowned. While I was swimming underwater, a corpse washed over to us from a small rock island. I was shivering with cold from the seawater and my balls had shrunk up, but I went with my friends to where people were forming a crowd. Someone shoved aside the strawmat covering the body. It was horrid. The corpse had no head. It was so waterlogged, we couldn't tell anything about its sex or age. Even now, when I think of that corpse, I can clearly recall the prominent blue vein on the thigh that looked like a waterlogged earthworm. But the reason I remember that day as if it were some personal day of commemoration is because it was an historical day. If it weren't for that, I would just remember it as some spring day when I happened to go swimming, so ridiculously early in the year, and saw a corpse.

But because of what was achieved by the April 19th Revolution, the day became unforgettable. So it turned out that I remember very clearly the date, the sea, and the corpse. I was so young then that, when I thought about my swimming in the same water where a headless corpse was floating around, I began to feel nauseated, and as my head swam with the strange horror of it, I rushed home. Ever since then, whenever April 19th comes around, I am reminded of the sea that day and of the corpse. Judging by the corruption of the corpse, it was easy to guess that it had had nothing to do with the April 19th Revolution.

But what is at issue was that I considered the Revolution of April 19th and the corpse to be inseparable. So the events of that day are ingrained in me as a decapitated corpse. My reasoning tells me that there was no relationship between April 19th and the corpse. As if to prove that rational thinking has no influence on what we like or dislike, I accepted the events of that day as being connected to one thing. During the April 19th Revolution, someone was killed at sea by decapitation. And I swam in the same ocean with the corpse.

What had happened to the head? Was it at the bottom of the dark sea, rolling its eyeballs and lamenting the fact that it could not move because it had no body? I was so extremely afraid of bizarre and strange things that I used to be unable to fall asleep after watching movies like *Dracula*. But I was becoming possessed by wild imaginings such as these. If the head was in the sea, sea cucumbers or octopuses must have sucked out the eyeballs, or whatever. Perhaps a baby octopus was having sweet dreams, curled up inside the empty skull. I am sure it was.

The waters on the east coast of Korea are already cold by mid-August. Since it was at the end of August, I thought we would not have the opportunity to go into the water. So when I answered "Of course" to her question as to whether we would be able to swim, I wasn't really thinking. My psychological approach to things was to avoid creating a negative atmosphere. Besides that, we didn't have much to talk about, as was true in that dark room. At a rest-stop at Daegwallyeong, we had coffee in paper cups and I wondered why I was ever holding a hot cup of coffee, since I usually disliked coffee and it was in the heat of the summer. Then we went through the so-called "Ninety-Nine Bends" of the Daegwallyeong Pass Road. In certain respects, we might have looked like a man and a woman just sitting side by side, without any special relationship. We probably did not even have that kind of tension between us.

The sea was quite calm. As the young frolicked in the water, the sea appeared to pulsate with them. It was a celebrated beach, but definitely past its peak, as the newspaper showed. Groups of people were scattered about on the sand, but—was it due to the thin sunlight?—there was only a handful of people whom one could count at a glance actually in the water. Looking out at the sea through the pine forest, we walked up the street, which was lined with places to lodge and to eat.

"Where shall we go? Are you hungry? Shall we first look for a place to stay?" I asked, somewhat embarrassed.

"Sure, whatever you like."

She had a way of looking at new things with a marvelous curiosity and was looking intently at the ocean through the pines. Her gaze showed she intended not to miss anything. —"Please come in!"

—"Of course, we serve meals." There were either skates or stingrays floundering like flared skirts in the fish tanks. I had studied philosophy in college in order to live a proper life, but I never acquired the wisdom to distinguish between skates and stingrays. Given the necessity to distinguish between Plato and Aristotle in order to reach love, our goal of life, it must also be necessary to differentiate between skates and stingrays.

"Let's first get a place to stay. Makes more sense," I mumbled, almost to myself.

I could not make up my mind about our life together. There was no guarantee that our living together would continue on into marriage. In fact, I felt that it shouldn't. It was her rented room. When I crept into her room, I had said rather brazenly, "I'll pay for our board and help out, too." What did I mean, "help out"? I was selfish then, and I am now. And I have to confess that my selfishness played a large part in why we lived together. I took it for granted that we would have to part and go our own way at some point. So I was careful to make sure that I did not become too close to her, living with her in the same room—indeed, that I better not become too close or attached to her.

Was it that I didn't like her? No, this was not the case. We would someday come to separate and each go our own way, but if that was not possible, we could just continue to live together. But, then, what was this nonsense? I was just continuing my uncertain life. I was afraid of certainty, of a revelation clearly laid out.

♥

When I think back about our relationship, I am reminded of the day that we went to visit my mother. My mother had a look at her but did not say a thing, one way or the other. Perhaps because of the gloomy weather, her room was dark and ponderous, like the inside of a tumulus. I knew that it wasn't just the weather. We had moved several times because of buying and selling our houses, but my mother's room was always like that. She would sit in the unlit room, staring into the darkness, even when the day was over. I never felt that my mother was death itself. It was just that she, and whatever pet she had (she always kept a cat as a companion), seemed like something people might bury alive with the dead. Occasionally, I would shudder in this atmosphere as the darkness she stared into seemed to writhe.

In some measure, my mother appeared to be reciting incantations, to breathe spirit into the energy that circulated in the darkness. Overwhelmed by my mother's power, my friend cowered awkwardly, sitting quietly next to me. Even if my friend were to become her daughter-in-law, my mother would not try to make much of her role as mother-in-law and would not have much to say. So I was busy trying to figure out how we might quickly take our leave after an exchange of a few words. I was hoping to free myself permanently from my mother's writhing darkness. I slid forward the bundle that held the gift I had brought for her.

"What's this?" Mom finally looked at me. I was ready to take whatever ire my present might bring forth. I just might have put together a gift that would make my parting from her more final.

"Open it later, when I'm gone," I said, as if it were nothing; but I was nervous. How sick I was to expect compensation from doing something so unexpected!

You can tell I was nervous, because I had been telling my friend, up until just before we went to see my mother, that I was an orphan. I had felt much safer saying that I was an orphan rather than otherwise. I sometimes felt that I could spit on the fact that I was not an orphan.

My feelings about my mother were all uncertain. They were all topsy-turvy. Sometimes, I pictured her waddling, as if her feet were bound, or at times as a beetle hiding itself in its shell. I avoided looking her squarely in the face. She probably felt the same way.

My mother had always been cold to me. Although her coldness wounded me, even before that, I had grown up nurturing•self-pity and regret at her early widowhood. I must have become vindictive once I decided to go live with a woman. I could never have anticipated that I would pay a visit to my mother with a gift. I was really confused, remembering the inescapable embarrassment I felt towards her.

When I had literally dragged my friend to go see my mother, despite the fact that I had told her I was an orphan, she must have been a little frightened. She became talkative.

"How old is she? Is she young?"

I did not even bother to answer such useless questions.

"What is it? Fabric for a dress?" She seemed very curious about the contents of the package I was holding at my side. I did not want to tell her.

"Anyway, all we have to do is just say hello," I said bluntly as we turned the corner before my house.

It is not easy to clarify the meaning that underlay my action. Even if there wasn't any outright consciousness of what I was doing, treachery was there, lurking in my long-suppressed emotions. If my encountering my mother came through her having given birth to me, it was possible that I had to rationalize the need for something quite comparable to it to make my parting from her more final. I had stuck the gift under my arm as if expecting that someone might snatch it from me, and had followed the labyrinthine alley as it climbed up. We had been living in the house for some time, since the real estate market had become depressed after we moved there. As the labyrinth grew steep, it also became quite cramped, allowing the passage of only a single person at a time. The long, narrow alleyway seemed like a snake slithering its way down. Finally, it would end like the tail of a snake. I would always become caught up in such thinking whenever I went there. This was particularly true whenever

I had to crawl back after having wandered around for a while and run out of money. Every time I came in, my mother, looking coldly at me, would say, "Isn't it about time you earned a living for yourself?"

It was true. I had nothing but dark habits acquired over the long span of a vagrant life. For a time, I used to have a severe inferiority complex, because I had only three negligible knife wounds. In those days, this kind of inferiority complex provided me with my only haven. In subsequent years, when I became a door-to-door salesman peddling all kinds of merchandise to make a living, I used to miss my days of feeling inferior for having only three knife scars. It's funny I should have felt like that.

The reason I was so taken aback as I entered the alleyway thinking I was entering the mouth of a snake was definitely not because the road became crooked and narrow. It had more to do with fear itself. I have touched a snake before, but I can't really tell you how its cold blood circulates through its body. Anyway, what I felt as I entered the alley was the chill of a snake. As if suffering from a groin pull, I crouched low and climbed toward the house, unconsciously muttering to myself in a stream, "Damn snake, damn snake!" Every time I had run away from home, I never dreamed of going back, unless because of something disastrous. My impulse to curse, which came out as "Damn snake!," had long been growing in me. I had long been suffering from that obsession. Although I was suffering, this doesn't mean that I got used to it. I was like a wild animal that defies taming. Coming and going from the house every day, I would always be surprised at how chillingly frightened I was and be overwhelmed by it. So, no one will find it odd that I had tried to run away five times before I graduated from high school. When I could no longer endure the cold and hunger and went back home with shoulders drooping, my mother would openly show her contempt with a look in her eye that said, "Where the hell else can you go?"

Out loud she said, "You're as useless as an acorn in a dog's bowl!"

Rather than what she said, it was the tone of her voice that was so chilling. When Mr. Kim, the man who was to arrange the sale of our house, was around, her tone was even more cutting and cold. She might have been less concerned with my running away from home than with my absence, which was even more pronounced, something she disliked. I don't think Mr. Kim ever felt ill-at-ease with me. He was always kind, as if he wore a mask painted with a kind expression. So when I imagined him even looking kindly at me in the dark, it scared me. After I started loitering in the street at night to avoid my homework, he still looked kindly upon me. When my truancy was discovered and the school asked my guardian to appear, he came to school as an uncle, in place of my mother, who said that she was ill and could not come. Even that night, he was kind to me.

After coughing dryly a few times to clear his throat, he called me over and said rather bluntly, "Maybe life is like the sound a frog makes jumping into an ancient, moss-filled pond. In the Japanese haiku ..."

I did not know what he was talking about. I could not tell whether he was saying that one should live one's life in any way one wants, because life is so empty and mysterious, or the opposite. I just bristled, wondering whom he meant by the Japanese, and what a haiku was. It was much later that I learned he meant the famous Japanese poet, Matsuo Bashō, and I was rather touched by it. The sound of a frog leaping into an ancient pond!

Speaking of foreign languages, he often spoke to my mother in Chinese, so that I would not understand what they were talking about. When that happened, I was the miserable child who had lost his father before being born.

Once, emboldened by drunkenness, I protested: "Why are you guys speaking in a different language?"

My mother cut me off: "You're drunk. Go to bed!"

Her sharp voice sounded metallic. My brazen protest was simply overpowered by it. Mr. Kim looked at me with some amusement, but in my mother's case, she could not have been colder. I was overwhelmed by these two very different expressions, and retreated to my room. Afterwards I rationalized my delinquency all the more, and whenever I felt that I was up to no good, I would scream the harder, imagining their faces.

Not long after that, I left home for the last time. I was wrapped up in a fantasy, that I would seek poetry and my father. Poetry and my father? I smiled, but I could not rid myself of the fantasy. I had heard that my father had died in China, but I was not at all interested in what had happened to him. When I truly started writing poetry, I wrote at the end of a poem entitled, "The Song of a Shoulder Blade in Northern Manchuria": *In the deep soil of that forgotten field, buried but not to be forgotten, a fragment of my father's shoulder blade must still be twittering away.* I left home in this mood, but not long afterwards, I had to go back again. Because I had met her. She had a tiny body, like a bird's. I was reminded of the Korean proverb that says, "Though small, a sparrow has many babies." After much thought, I decided I should go back home. I wanted to show off in some way that I had become self-sufficient.

A greater hostility seemed to have impregnated the house. I held my breath as I reached for the front gate and gently pushed it. The gate was barred. I hesitated, biting my lip. I knew it would be locked. Even so, confirming it, I went limp. The old framework of the gate had labels posted on it showing the meter readings for water and electricity, phone numbers of movers, and an arrow drawn with chalk indicating the downhill side of the road. As if expecting to discern something important in them, I examined each of them carefully.

I couldn't turn back.

So I went up to the gate and pushed my hand into a crack on the right. I had almost forgotten about it. I could feel the string at the end of my hand. The bar could be pulled aside by pulling the string. As if removing a stitch from a sutured wound, I pulled the string with some apprehension. Click. The bar was aside at the small click. I was vividly reminded of the times I had been so nervous, worrying that the bar would make a racket when it was opened. How was I going to greet my mother? I had no idea: I might as well have been standing in the middle of a desolate field. I could practically hear her asking coldly, "What brings you here?"

It occurred to me that someone might be looking out a window. I quietly stepped away to a spot out of the line of sight from the room. Since I was fearful enough to be cautious even when turning a page at night, I tried to keep a lid on things by being stealthy. I was so excessively careful that it had become my habit to behave like a cornered animal which retreats with its tail tucked between its legs and with fear in its eyes. No one should be surprised that I ran away at night. Like a well-mannered man who goes wild once he puts on his reserve uniform, a thing that changes him from an individual to a member of a group, the darkness of the night had the power to transform me from a person into a member of a group. From this point of view, half the world in the dark must be a blessing for both the brave and timid alike.

However, I simply cannot blame the fearfulness that kept me even from turning a page.

I had been vaguely thinking that my mother, like a magician, had the old ghost trapped in perpetual sleep in a jar and thought that I should never make a noise that might wake it up. When you are young, you are always curious about how an older person remembers things. I had never known what my mother thought of my deceased father. Somehow, there was not even a hint of what she thought, so far as I could see, which made me think that she must have met my father simply to bear me. Who knows whether her memories had struggled to present themselves as huge as a dinosaur or as hard and small as a beetle, and yet ended up trapped in her versatile net. I kept an eye on her with such thoughts in mind, but she seemed as completely natural as an old fox with nine tails. But it was difficult to believe that my mother had completely erased her past from her memory. On occasion, what she unconsciously said proved that. She remembered the smallest details of her past.

"Chinese moon-cake is sweeter than this."

Mom was definitely recalling the past as she tasted a bit of mooncake I had bought in a Chinese store and brought to her. So when she was looking completely serene like an old fox, I had an impulse to lift her skirt to see how her nine tails were, and to wonder what she looked like when she slept with Mr. Kim at night.

Once, I went back home, and, like a thief casing the house, I hid myself. Just then, something quickly passed by in front of me and I heard a meowing. That's when I bumped into my mother. She was just raising herself from a stooped position.

"Your leg … is it bothering you a lot?"

Instead of saying hello, I asked this, looking at her prosthetic leg. I could see she was getting back to normal.

"You … you came home. You scared the cat." She didn't answer my question but spoke in an intonation that was devoid of emotion. Her tone of voice seemed weak in spite of her intention to be deliberately cold. I stared at her as if checking to see whether she had suddenly aged. Of course, she didn't look at all changed. But what had happened to her air of dreadful fierceness? Suddenly I realized—and it must have been right—that my mother had sensed that I had caught her looking at her own prosthetic leg in a corner of the yard (not even in her room) and cursing her own life, full of regret. She seemed to feign helplessness. Like a beetle pretending to be dead when touched.

"Let's go inside." She tried not to show her limp.

"Oh, no. I don't need to."

"Why not?" She looked at me, curious.

"No," I said firmly, once again. I imagined a faint smile passing over her lips like a wilted petal.

"There's no one here."

"No. That's not it."

"Then, what is it?"

"Something's come up … and I need some money." I just said it as though, no matter what she might say, I had no choice.

"Money?"

My mother looked disappointed, as if to say, "Oh, that's it," but she nodded slightly, perhaps resigned. However, she did not say what I expected to hear: "The loser, in trouble again." It didn't seem possible that she was the same mom who had labeled me an "acorn in a dog's bowl." She seemed quite changed. I made up an excuse, saying that I had to enroll in a foreign-language institute and needed money. She just listened. She did not seem to care whether I was telling the truth or not. I was afraid that she saw straight through me, as if into a cleft chicken. I stressed how much I needed it. After listening to me for a while, she slowly turned to me and said she understood.

"I don't have any money now … but, here, take this…."

She said nothing else. She twisted the gold ring from her finger. I can't say for sure whether I was happy or sad just then.

"It's two ounces."

Her voice seemed to come out of a long tube. Everything seemed hazy, as if I were under a spell. If the two ounces of pure gold had changed into something else, it might have been an alloy of my joy at having fooled my mother and gotten some money, and of my confusion which arose when my mother took off her ring and gave it to me without a hint of contempt. I had never felt such mixed emotions. It didn't seem right that my mother should accommodate me so easily. I could not figure out what sort of incantation the ring had.

I left the house feeling unsettled. Dusk was already gathering. When I met my friend that night, I unexpectedly suggested that we live together. Had my mother screamed at me and poured out her contempt on me, there's no doubt that the situation would have been very different. I seemed to be moving in opposite directions, like a toy puppet raising its arms when the strings are pulled down.

My plan to give my mother a new prosthetic leg as a gift has to be understood along this line of thinking. Her prosthetic leg was always a mystery to me. I had never seen her take it off. One summer, when her leg was exposed, I happened to see that the prosthesis went up to her shin. She was almost obsessive about not showing it. I always wondered what she did when she went to bed. Whenever I saw Mr. Kim, I was dying to ask him about it. I didn't know what kind of feelings he had toward my mother, whether he merely pitied her or what. I knew that he had a family of his own, yet he never left my mother's side. He was like her hands and feet. It seemed that she stood on her prosthetic leg and on one of Mr. Kim's.

In this regard, her leg, which had been amputated because of an injury she suffered during a Japanese military riot, and the Japanese allusions that Mr. Kim perpetually made in every conversation, seemed to make for a gloomy contradiction. In reality, the more I hated my mother, the more I became possessed by the ghosts of the Voluntary Service Corps, the "Comfort Women." I came to believe that my mother had volunteered for the Service Corps and had returned after enduring extreme hardships. Since so many young women had lost their lives, there was no point in ascribing much tragic significance to the loss of her leg. Occasionally, I thought about such things and enjoyed such miserable imaginings, like some boy immersed in his evil thoughts.

My mother did not allow visits from close relatives. Unless it was something big, of course. Partly because of the discomfort of her leg, she would stay at home all day like a hen, sitting cross-legged. In the dark room of her tumulus, Mr. Kim was the only passageway to the world. Mom bought and sold her houses according to his recommendations. If it weren't for the fact that he spent the night with her, he would have seemed like her agent. If a cat got sick and died, or got old and left home, it was his duty to get a new kitten. It didn't seem that she was making any special requests of him. I would never have figured out what her real feelings were toward him had she not cried during an argument with him. One evening, when I went to bed especially early, my ears pricked up at hearing her arguing with Mr. Kim. At first, I thought it was coming from a neighbor's house. There were low voices and then suddenly the house reverberated with shouting. I didn't know what it was about, but both of them were arguing about something that had gone wrong. I was so anxious that I held my breath and turned off the light. At that moment, I realized that my mother was not only cold to me, but was also very cold to Mr. Kim, according to circumstances. After a while, I heard Mr. Kim throw open the door with a loud thud and come out of the room.

"I will never come back!"

He was fuming. He must have been quite angry, even though I could only imagine him smiling.

"Do whatever you want!"

My mother had replied as if caving in. Mr. Kim had apparently stepped down from the hall and was opening the storage cabinet where his shoes were, so he could put them on. I could feel the heightened tension between him and my mother.

At last, Mr. Kim walked up to the gate. Just then, my mother ran out, following after him. But the gate had already banged shut behind him. That night I heard her sobbing in her room. Thinking he would never return, I had a taste of inexplicable emptiness. But I had guessed wrong. He was back within a day.

♥

When my friend and I entered the room, my mother had her cat with her. After I introduced her to my mother, I gave Mom the present.

"What is it?" She grabbed it, ignoring my words to open it after we were gone, and opened it right there.

"Oh, no. This is ..." It must have taken her by surprise, for she was aghast. A tremor passed across her face as if across the scales of a snake.

"I ordered one from the store you used to go to." I pretended that it was nothing.

"What an unpredictable rascal you are!" my mother said. She seemed to groan, even though my friend was there. Then she grabbed the passing cat and stroked it under the neck. I was determined not to be concerned about her feelings, even if they were hurt. I considered the whole thing to be an act which would confirm my separation from her, and therefore I thought it her fate, however she might take it. Her hand seemed to grow stronger with greed as she stroked the cat. The cat struggled to break her grip.

"I was expecting this to happen." The cat slipped away. "I've had mine for so long, I was getting sick and tired of it. It's a good thing you got me a new one."

With this casual remark, she turned away and started untying her artificial leg. It was tied on above the thigh. I had not sought to bring about such a scene. Why was she doing this? I looked at my friend and signaled that she should be patient, even though she might be uncomfortable with what was going on. When my mother turned back, she held the prosthetic leg in her hand. It looked as though it had just been sawed off. She had paled, but appeared to have transcended this world of glory and shame, like a widow buried with her dead husband.

"I've had this for a long time. I'm going to give it to you, since you've gotten me a new one. I was going to do it some day, anyway."

"What do you mean?" I asked in surprise.

"When you used to leave the house, I felt empty because I had no one to hate. I've always needed someone to hate, ever since your father died. There's been no one but you to hate. I didn't have anyone I could trust." She spoke as if casting a spell.

I felt the dull blow of a heavy hammer to my head.

"When I heard that he was failing, I went to him immediately. I had to travel a long distance. I had been waiting so desperately for news of him. It was … it was to a place called Jang-ga-goo, at the beginning of summer. Jang-ga-goo, Zhangjiakou…." Her voice was uneven. Her breath shortened, as if she were trying to control herself.

"It was the provincial capital of Caiha'er Province, deep inside the continent. It was also an entryway through the Great Wall of China. From there, you pass through Ningxia and Liaozhou and get onto the southern road, in Tianshan. You arrive in the faraway Western Region, through the Gansu Corridor."

My mother narrated this as if she were reciting an incantation. She actually appeared to be possessed by a spirit. Perhaps from having said "faraway," she seemed to be somewhere far-off. I, too, let out something of a sigh:

"Ah, the Western Region … So you went there?"

I was a little confused by how many place-names there were, but I remembered hearing "Western Region" very clearly. For she had brought it up several times in the past. Her eyes glistened, blue like phosphate.

"I only got as far as Zhangjiakou. From there to the Western Region is about seven times the distance between Seoul and Pusan."

"That, indeed, is very far."

"Of course."

"What happened then?"

"When I reached their base in Zhangjiakou, I heard what had happened to your father. He had already passed away. A lady named Chui told me."

My mother began to gasp, as if out of breath. I could not understand her.

"I don't understand what you're saying." I shook my head.

"I don't understand it, either. I would not have blamed him so much, had I known all the circumstances. And you, too.... He waited for me so desperately, but he had to leave Zhangjiakou. By then, he was almost dead."

"But why did he have to take off again?"

"No one knows why. According to Chui, he said he had to leave, even if it meant he would die soon."

"Who was this Chui?"

"She was acting as your father's wife. For money, she pretended to be his wife. It was she who sent me the telegram that he was in critical condition. She told me that he was indeed critically ill. But no one could stop him from taking off for the Western Region."

"Why the Western Region?"

"I don't know." She sighed deeply. I thought, "Maybe my father had a bad case of wanderlust," but I didn't say it. I thought there must have been some reason why, even sick, he could not avoid dragging himself off on a journey.

"But open this ... This is the only legacy from your father. I received it from Chui ... I don't know how I managed to hang onto it, even when I lost my leg because of enemy fire as I was leaving Zhangjiakou." She pushed the artificial leg toward me. I didn't know what she was doing. She even grinned at me.

"There's a lid at the center, where the bone should be."

"A lid?" I held up the prosthetic leg, carefully examining it. Indeed, there was a little lid shaped like a bottle cap at the center of the leg. It looked like a fragment of severed bone. I placed my thumb and forefinger on it and turned it to the left with a slight push. It turned easily. What came out, to my surprise, was a roll of paper. I trembled as if I were performing some secret rite of a shaman's disciple.

"What is this?"

"Unroll it." My mother, too, sounded excited.

My friend was squatting in the corner, not making a peep, intently watching the whole ritual with a frightened look in her eyes.

When I unrolled it, I saw lettering.

"It's your father's handwriting. Look at the very beginning."

"This is ..."

"Right. You don't know how many times I've read it. For a long time ... I kept it where it would be as safe as could be. It is a record of his feelings which he jotted down whenever he was moved to do so, but it has given me a sense of peace whenever I read it. Read the other side, too."

"Okay."

Closing her eyes, she started to recite what was on the paper. The part she recited was the preface, so to speak. She recited it for a long while. Even I could perceive the gravity of her emotions, although they were new to me. As she recited, the place-names she had mentioned came up. She must have drawn them from memory when she told me about them.

> "... How can a man commit an act shameful before heaven? Triple-peaked, treacherous Taebaek Mountain looms high above us and never changes, even after ten- thousand years. I, too, who am traveling to a desolate land, will achieve my goal, even if I live on wind and sleep on the dew."

It did not say what his goal was. I looked at my mother, holding onto my seriousness. She had brightened up like a little girl. I felt myself choking up. I felt as though it had been for this moment that I had been so hostile to my mother and she to me. I felt as though I understood everything. How I had longed for my mother and how must she have longed to accept me!

"Your father was trying to flee from the Japanese military."

"Fleeing ... from the Japanese military ... to the West!" I stammered. Many Koreans had been taken to China, having been forcefully drafted into the Japanese military. I, too, knew that quite a few had fled.

"So, when did you meet my son?"

In response, my friend began to squirm, as if suddenly shy, which was not typical of her, and she turned red. This is what led to our living together.

♥

And how much time had passed since then? We finally came to the beach. We climbed up a considerable distance past the restaurants and the lodges. Without ever communicating what we each were interested in seeking, we both had our eyes on a building far in the distance. We both had poor eyesight, but both of us must have known that, clearly, it was an inn. It was right next to the ocean on the other side of the road. The pines had long ended, and the winding road to the beach suddenly changed into a typical country road. The sea was quite close. The waves shone white, like the small teeth of a beached whale. The inn stood quite by itself. It wasn't in any way special with regard to its facilities, nor did it have an air of belonging to a class apart. The building was quite old and appeared rundown; even the paint on the sign was peeling.

In spite of this, we headed for that inn. I thought it must have been the proximity of the building to the sea, so we could listen to the sound of the waves for a lullaby. The inn was old and its amenities were nothing to look at, but I felt I would be very disappointed if we were not taken in. I took the absence of any objection from her to mean she agreed with what I was thinking.

At that moment, I caught sight of a small patch of green onions in a corner of the inn, which seemed very out-of-character. A few of the stems had flowers that looked like the balls on a plane tree. It would be an exaggeration to think of it as a garden of green onions. Someone must have grown the green onions for his own consumption and a few of them had ended up blooming. I looked at the greenish-white flowers, recalling that they bloom in the springtime.... Because green onions are harvested before they bloom, one rarely sees their flowers unless, of course, one wants to collect the seeds.

I started to think about our life together as I looked at the flowers. She hated green onions. Occasionally, we used to go to a bone-marrow soup shop and order a bowl of *seol-leong-tang* for each of us. She would take her chopsticks and remove all the finely sliced green onions floating in the soup. I would tell her that eating *seol-leong-tang* without green onions was like eating *naeng-myon* without vinegar and mustard. But she would not listen. All her green onions ended up in my bowl. I was the exact opposite. I had to heap loads of green onions in my soup. She said the reason she disliked green onions was because they made her sleepy; she couldn't move. Slicing an onion made her eyes heavy.

"This reminds me of *Hôtel du Nord*."

The stairs leading to the upstairs were squeaky. It seemed natural that she would be reminded of the small edition of the novel, *Hôtel du Nord*, that she had read some time ago. It made her think of an old, dilapidated hotel. The second story seemed to have been an addition, made of wood. The place was in poor condition. When we got to our room, we did not sit down, but just stood there for a while. The floor was sandy. When we asked the clerk why everything was so neglected, he answered tersely that the place was going to be torn down soon, for redevelopment. So it was practically an abandoned building.

"Isn't it better? We'll never come back to this place." She seemed more contented.

"Let's go out. We need to get a bite to eat."

I pushed the suitcases to one side. Now that we had the room, I wanted to get out of there, hungry or not.

We backtracked along the road we had come on, after we left the inn. Evening was already in the air. Why had we come to the sea after the season was over? A look at the miserable room in the inn made me think this. Someday, we will have to part. To do this, we will need some kind of an occasion. We had never adjusted to one another and continued to live together for a long time, without it meaning anything. It was life in a morass. Although both of us felt that we could not take a step forward, neither of us was able to bring up the subject. When I stepped into that room, I realized that, now, this would be the end. The minute we returned to Seoul, we would forget the past as if suffering from amnesia, and go on with our lives as if we had never met. I bit my lip hard. But I had no plan as to what I would do afterwards, or how. It was clear that we must make our parting a new departure and a new beginning.

"Isn't this a seasnail?" she asked in a lively tone, looking into a plastic tub under a faucet.

"Yeah. Shall we ask for two of them?" I took one out of the water. The seasnail pulled back, deep into its shell. She tapped the seasnails in the tub and was having fun, like a child, watching them retract into their shells. Did this woman have such a side, too? It was like seeing someone new, not the woman I had lived with for so long. At the same time, I was reminded of the strange story of a sea snail that turned into a bird. It was Jeong Yak-jeon of the Joseon period who said that a thousand-year-old seasnail turns into a blue bird. Scientifically speaking, it does not make sense. A seasnail could never turn into a bird. But it suddenly occurred to me that if a thousand years does not just refer to a thousand years, but was meant to indicate some indefinite time, no one could say for sure that a seasnail might not turn into a bird.

In the theory of evolution, apes evolved into human beings, and if we go even further back, all land animals evolved from sea creatures. In so-called fossils of the archaeopteryx, sharp claws like those of an animal's paws were found on their wings. So, the front paws of quadrupeds became wings. We find it hard to believe that a mouse would turn into a bird. But bats can fly, even though they are not birds. From this standpoint, it is not so strange that a seasnail might turn into a bird after a few hundred-million years, and fly around.

"They say that a seasnail will turn into a bird if it gets very, very old," I said with a serious face while our food was being served.

"A bird?"

"Yeah."

"A bird with wings?"

"Are there birds without wings?" I finally smiled.

"You're kidding." She smiled, too.

"No, I'm not. Can you imagine that a white grub becomes a cicada?"

"I've never seen a white grub."

Of course, she could have said so, even if she had seen one. I knew that she was an utterly blank page when it came to animal and plant life. If she saw a flat beetle come into the room, she would think it was a baby turtle.

"If you didn't know what a white grub is, imagine a tadpole becoming a frog."

"There's nothing strange about that. It's only natural."

I could not go on with the conversation. A seasnail becoming a bird over a long time was not the same thing as a tadpole becoming a frog. Even if, in some distant future, a seasnail were to turn into a bird through some strange, biological mutation, it would have nothing to do with us. We will not be here in a few decades, let alone a few hundred-million years. Pushing a spoonful of rice into my mouth, I said, "Anyhow, they said it turns into a bird. A blue bird," and went back to chewing my food. Actually, I was terribly grateful to her that she didn't break out with some line like "My ear is a seashell. It longs to hear the sound of the waves ..." when she saw the seasnail. I didn't want our parting ornamented with such corny verse.

A thousand-year-old seasnail will turn into a bird.

The reason I brought up such a ridiculous tale must have been because I wanted to discombobulate her imagination. But it was all useless. Even if the seasnails in the tub were to change into some red or yellow birds just then, rather than off in the distant future, and fly away, what relevance would it have for our life? The only thing that I had to take charge of was how to pull it off in a natural way.

"The intestines taste the best." I picked up a black portion of the seasnail, which came out twisted like a little hat.

"Isn't it bitter?"

"No, it's nutty."

Her chopsticks went to the raw fish. We didn't talk much after that. Only the noisy whir of the fan filled the restaurant.

When we left the restaurant, it was dark. We went back to the inn, strolling along the road that seemed to be a long dyke. In the dark, the inn looked even more dilapidated and set in the autumn, while everything else still lingered in the summer heat. Like renters about to be evicted, we picked up the key and climbed the squeaking stairs to the second floor. It seemed we were the only guests.

"It feels as if we've come a few thousand miles," she said, opening the curtains in the room. I felt the same way. We had just traveled about five hours by bus, and there's no place that far away in this small country. But why did we feel we had traveled several thousand miles? Outside the window, the ocean was turning a deep green in the dark, and the waves were breaking faintly at the edge of it. Well, now I really had to figure out how to leave her. Hesitating, I went over to the adjoining bathroom and turned on the water in the tub. Rusty water gushed from the spout. I stood there completely lost, my hands in my pockets. Right from the first, I had never planned to get in the bathtub, even if the water were clean. I realized just then that I was out of cigarettes.

Hurriedly turning around, I told her that I had to go buy cigarettes. She looked at me as if she had not understood. She must have heard me wrong.

"I have to go buy some cigarettes. There's only a few left," I said, as if begging for forgiveness.

"Won't they have some, downstairs?" She was telling me the store would be too far away.

"They won't have any. Did you see that the water doesn't work properly? Damn!"

I rushed out of the room, grumbling. She was well aware that I became extremely anxious and could not bear it if I ran out of cigarettes. Even if it were midnight and I was just ready to go to bed, if I found my pack of cigarettes running low, I would run off to a tobacco shop. The cigarette shop was on the street with all the restaurants, including the one where we had had the seasnails. The late evening breeze was quite refreshing as I came out of the inn. I walked quickly. I had come out to buy cigarettes and the store was quite far, but I felt very light, as if I had been freed from some oppression. It was the sense of liberation from that inn, where she was. I was astonished at the sense of freedom I felt. It was incomprehensible. It was an emotion that I had never felt before. I even thought it hilarious that I had been wanting to leave her so desperately. I went away from the inn as if I were running away.

♥

It happened in my childhood. While growing up in a seaside town, I happened to be playing with a neighborhood girl on the beach. I don't remember everything that happened that day, but we spent the whole day playing in the sand after we had gone into the water completely naked Psychologists talk about children having periods when they play in the sand or in the dirt, and it must have been one of those times with us, too. We spent hours building castles with wet sand and then tearing them down. Suddenly, she had said, "The sun is setting." Indeed, the round, red sun was setting behind the hills. We were in big trouble. We had to get home quickly. We stood up. But then what happened? We could not find the place where we had hidden our clothes. We had made the mistake of hiding our clothes in the sand before we went into the water. But we had made a small mound and marked it clearly. We were terrified. We dug up every possible place, but our clothes were nowhere to be found. We wandered along the beach, naked and in tears. The more we wandered, the more difficult it became to find the place where our clothes were buried. When it got dark, we were both in tears, sniveling. We kept wandering along the beach. If the grown-ups had not come looking for us, we might have spent the night that way.

I walked along the beach remembering all this. The sea, sunken in the darkness, seemed to sway, slow and heavy. There seemed to be no moon. The waves that had been breaking white, only seemed to come up occasionally, like the fin of some dark fish. Electric lights in the distance shone like bug zappers. I strolled along in the darkness. When I turned to look back at the inn, pale florescent light was pouring out of a lone room on the second floor. It was light from a different world, off in the distance. Suddenly impelled, I started taking off my clothes. This wasn't just because I was remembering old times. I walked about, completely naked. It is said that the naked body is more invisible in the dark than one that is clothed. I walked about freely, as if I had become an invisible man. I felt as if I had become truly free, having escaped from every form of bondage. I strolled around on the deserted beach like an animal that had just evolved from a fish.

Suddenly, the sound of the waves grew loud, and the sky was filled with birds. The seasnails had become birds. As they flew, their eyes twinkled like the distant stars. The thousand-year-old seasnails that had been transformed. The seasnails that had soared into the sky from the bottom of the sea after an upheaval brought on by a typhoon. The seasnails that were several hundred-million years old. The freedom of having won their wings and of having discarded their shells.

Not long after, she married another man. Not long after: It was two months and ten days, if you want to be exact. This is to say, she, too, dreamed of parting, just as I had. When I returned to the room, led by a police officer, my middle barely covered, she had fallen asleep, leaning against the wall.

Sometime later, I had occasion to read the poem "Loulan" by Gim Chunsu. It was composed of difficult sections, such as "Gebitan" and "Mt. Mingsha Shan." I halted in "Mingsha Shan." In it, I found lines like these:

> *On the far side of Mount Mingsha Shan, it rains once every ten years. When it does rain, white onion flowers bloom here and there in the rocky fields. Loulan, a land ready to wilt at any minute, so like the white blossoms of the onion.*

Loulan. There's no proof that my father ever went there. But I still imagined a man traveling into that land, west of China. Although I don't know how different onion flowers and green-onion flowers are, I thought of her, she who had found it so difficult to touch green onions, and of the inn, with its flowers of green onions. Loulan had been an oasis, but was now destroyed. The inn must have been torn down by then, leaving not a trace. That love had ended. It was yet still later that a female mummy was discovered in Loulan. The red silk cloth which covered the mummy bore the Chinese characters, "Immutable, for a Thousand Years." My heart ached upon reading this promise of a heart unchanging forever. But, of course, a mummy is nothing more than a mummy.

The country where the mummy was found and where the white flowers of the onion bloom. Is that what our encounter was? Are all such encounters of the world like that? Or, is it that even love, like a wasteland, harbors the secret orders of a certain Providence?

♥

About "The Love of Loulan"

This translation of fiction by the celebrated Korean writer Yun Humyong is to be applauded, and Cross-Cultural Communications is to be congratulated on making it available. Although there have been some significant translations from modern Korean literature, especially of poetry, we are surprisingly ignorant of the prose writing of a country which, after all, was the scene of the first major post-Second World War conflict. This narrative, expertly translated by Kim and Steffen Richards, is hypnotic in its detailed observation and at the same time attention to the flow of the story. At all points, the author relates natural phenomena, the closely observed natural world, to the inner life of his protagonists. A central image is that of the snake, and his narrative itself is serpentine in its twists and turns. Perfectly naturally it follows the thought processes of the speaker, with many diversions, doublings back, but never so as to detract from the ongoing direction or energy in the narrative. This work reminds me, to some extent, of the fiction of Isaac Bashevis Singer, which also flows in a perfectly natural way, without apparent artifice, although it is demonstrably extremely sophisticated. At no point does one feel that Yun Humyong is being self-indulgent, so that he—as author—pushes himself forward into the spotlight, so to speak, and stands there to be admired. At the same time, the reader is drawn more and more into the culture, the ambience of Korean life, not through obvious references or circumstantial detail of the kind that pop fiction relies upon, but through swift, subtle, and economically drawn allusion to cultural detail, above all to the folklore still so active in Korea. The asides, if they may be so called, are thus seamlessly embodied in the narrative, at the same time enriching it, but never, as I have said, calling undue attention to themselves. The narrative will tell one more about reality of life in Korea, in the post-April 19th Revolution period, than any contemporary history or journalistic account. Superficially reminiscent of contemporary American literature, it is at the same time quite distinct. The translators, in rejecting the temptation to naturalize this work of fiction, have afforded us a non-fiction insight into a culture with which many might feel it to be their duty to familiarize themselves.

—Daniel Weissbort

London, England
July 2005

Translators' Acknowledgments

We wish to express our appreciation to the many individuals and organizations that have made the translation and publication of this book possible. The Korea Literature Translation Institute has generously supported us in this regard. We salute their unfailing support of translations meant to help put Korean literature within reach of world readers. Ms. Eunhye Chu, Mr. Joong-ho Won, and Ms. Yana Kim, all of KLTI, have been especially helpful and steadfast in seeing us through our year-long project.

Our deep thanks go to the author, Yun Humyong, for his confidence and enthusiasm for the project. In translating this book, we have benefited greatly from *L'Amour de Dunhuang* (Ch'oe Yun and Patrick Murus's French translation of the same title). Many of our collegaues at the University of California at Berkeley—Ms. Ying Yang, Ms. Lihua Zhang, and Ms. I Hao Lee—gave generously of their time and expertise in helping us with the Romanization of Chinese names.

Last but not the least, we wish to thank Mr. Stanley H. Barkan, editor and publisher of Cross-Cultural Communications, for his appreciation of the text,, his meticulous attention to detail, and his vision of bringing world literature to the attention of readers everywhere.

—Kyung-nyun Richards
Steffen F. Richards

Berkeley, California
July 2005

About the Translators

Kyung-nyun Kim Richards is a poet and lecturer at U. C. Berkeley, where she teaches the Korean language. Steffen F. Richards, her husband, has a Master's degree in Oriental Languages from U. C. Berkeley and a background in translating from the Japanese; also a poet, he is a contributor to *Light, Dark Wind, Moon* (Aventine Press, 2004). Together, they have translated works by Yun Dong-ju (Asian Humanities Press, 2003), Kim Seung-hee (Homa & Sekey Publishers, 2004), and Kang Eun-kyo. Their book-length translation of the memoirs of Col. Kay In-ju is as yet unpublished. Kim Richards' translation of Theresa Hak-kyung Cha's *Dictée* into Korean, which was first published in 1997, was republished in 2004 by Omungak Publishers, Inc., in Seoul, Korea. Her original works have appeared in *Shim-sang / Poetry: Image and Criticism, San Francisco Moon-hak-ji* (literary Journals), and *San Francisco PEN Literature.* She contributes poems and essays to *The Korea Daily / JoongAng Ilbo* and *The Korea Times Daily / HanGook Ilbo,* both San Francisco editions. Both translators have been recipients of grants from the Korean Culture and Arts Foundation (1997-1998), the Korean Literature Translation Foundation (1998-1999), and the Korea Literature Translation Institute (2004-2005).

Kyung-nyun Kim Richards was the top prize winner of the Literature Translation Contest held by *The Korea Times* of the Republic of Korea (1996) and the recipient of a Commendation of the Prime Minister of the Republic of Korea for her contribution to the translation of Korean Literature (2004)

Kyung-nyun Kim Richards and Steffen F. Richards live in Berkeley, California, and have two grown children.